'It's you, isn't it? You're my runaway girl?'

Grant said again, not taking his eyes from her face.

'Yes...if you really must know,' Titia said, giving in. There was no point in keeping up the line.

'Why didn't you say so right away?' he persisted.

'I don't want to open old wounds,' Titia said with exasperation. 'There's no point dwelling on the past. No one else knows about it and I want to keep it that way.'

Rebecca Lang trained to be a State Registered Nurse in Kent, England, where she was born. Her main focus of interest became operating theatre work, and she gained extensive experience in all types of surgery on both sides of the Atlantic. Now living in Toronto, Canada, she is married to a Canadian pathologist and has three children. When not writing, Rebecca enjoys gardening, reading, theatre, exploring new places, and anything to do with the study of people.

Recent titles by the same author:

THE PERFECT TREATMENT

DIAGNOSIS DEFERRED

BY
REBECCA LANG

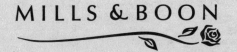

MILLS & BOON

First published in Great Britain 2000
Harlequin Mills & Boon Limited,
Eton House, 18-24 Paradise Road, Richmond, Surrey TW9 1SR

© Rebecca Lang 2000

ISBN 0 263 82234 6

Set in Times Roman 10½ on 12 pt.
03-0005-53910

Printed and bound in Spain
by Litografia Rosés, S.A., Barcelona

CHAPTER ONE

'HEY...lady...don't I know you? You sure look familiar!'

The deep, masculine voice spoke off to one side as Dr Laetitia Lane stood, holding open the heavy oak door to the aptly named Open Door clinic, watching the early morning patients and patrons straggle in off the street where they had been waiting since dawn. From the appearances of some, it was obvious that they had been sleeping rough.

Laetitia tensed, her green eyes widening. For a second or two her heart seemed to stop beating, then it started up again with a thump and an accelerated rate. Very deliberately she did not look in the direction of the voice, concentrating instead on the stream of people entering. It was not that she intended to ignore the man—she just needed time to steel herself.

It was an attractive voice, holding a hint of laughter and a teasing note, a voice that would not normally call a woman 'lady', she felt sure. It seemed familiar, yet it must be...eight years, she reflected, since she had heard it last. Now it sent a strange jolt of recognition through her which was both joyous and horribly doom-laden, a ghost from the past—a past she thought she had put behind her, an episode she would have sooner forgotten.

That *should* have been a welcome greeting at eight o'clock in the morning on a day that promised to be hectic, long and swelteringly hot, among other things. Life at the clinic was rewarding but never easy—a theatre

5

of the unexpected, one might say. As it was, she was not prepared for any sort of emotional confrontation, least of all that one.

'Morning, Tishy,' one of the men entering greeted her. He was one of her regulars. He had a battered face, and generally slept under a bush in the nearby park during the summer months. All his worldly goods, apart from the clothes he was wearing, he carried in an equally battered knapsack on his back. With the other street people who used the clinic and drop-in centre he shuffled in to go to the Eating Place where he would get a good cooked breakfast. Later he would have a shower, get a haircut, use the launderette to wash his clothes, see a doctor or a volunteer dentist.

'Morning, Dodge.' Laetitia smiled at him, finding that her throat was tight with emotions and she could scarcely get the words out, waiting for that other voice again. 'Good to see you again.' It *was* good to see the regulars and to know that they looked forward to seeing her.

'Likewise,' he replied, his gravelly voice indicating excessive smoking, as well as the ever-present low-grade chest infection which was a common hazard for street people.

In those few moments in which she spoke to Dodge, Laetitia's mind swept over the past—a past she thought she had purged—as one's eyes might have scanned a picture quickly, looking for the details, placing the owner of the voice there. After all he had done for her, she had only sent the one letter, thanking him. Shame did strange things to you. Yes…strangely, it was still there, that feeling of shame, the kind that made you shrivel up inside, frightened to acknowledge your identity. That was something she had in common with the people who entered the drop-in centre—most of them had something to hide, if only from themselves.

Often, over the eight years, she had wondered whether he had been trying to find her. Certainly, she had not made it easy for him—he didn't know her real name or where she lived. She had laid a false trail for him, if he had cared enough to follow any trail. Perhaps she had been flattering herself.

'Morning, Rita, morning Mac,' she greeted two others, forcing her mind back to the present moment.

'Morning, Doc.' They crowded past her, eager yet orderly, a motley crew of people moving towards the smells of freshly made coffee, frying bacon and toasting bread that wafted out from one of the many capacious anterooms of the Church of St Barnabas. Those smells mingled with the comforting scents of wood and floor polish.

Laetitia squared her shoulders. All that in the past was water under the proverbial bridge now. Life for her had been transformed. Composing her features, pushing back her coppery red hair from her forehead, which was already beaded with sweat from the summer heat, Laetitia turned her head slowly, a defiant gleam in her eye. She knew she looked different now…and not just her hair.

The man was standing on the bottom step of the wide oak stairway that went from street level, where she stood, up to the level of the main body of the church where the congregation of St Barnabas gathered on a Sunday. He was tall, slim, dark-haired, his hair shorter than it had been, and he was casually dressed in linen pants and an open-necked shirt. He looked older, too—he *was* older, of course, she reminded herself. She saw a good-looking, mature man, with laugh lines around his eyes and that expression which came from having seen a lot of the world, perhaps too much.

As their eyes met, Laetitia strove to make her expression as bland as possible, showing only mild curiosity, friendliness. Even so, she felt the pupils of her eyes widening, a flush of colour suffusing her cheeks, as another jolt of recognition went through her like an electric shock. Oh, my God…it definitely *is* him! The acknowledgment jarred her more than she had expected. She'd had a crush on him when she was sixteen, that was for sure.

'Hi…' He was coming towards her, his eyes narrowed, a hand outstretched to meet hers. As he got close to her, his glance swept over her astutely. 'I'm Grant Saxby…Dr Saxby, that is. You look like someone I used to know in my youth and haven't seen since.' He spoke casually, as though meeting her was all in a day's work.

'Oh?' Laetitia forced herself to smile, holding out her hand to him as he got close.

Even as she maintained the nonchalance, she was asking herself why she was doing it, pretending that she didn't know him. While the warmth of his touch seemed to surge through her, the explanatory words would not come. The sight of him brought back a gamut of mixed emotions, powerful and haunting, the pleasurable ones vying with the excruciatingly poignant. Damnation!

With his cool eyes he scrutinized her face, feature by feature, taking in her brilliant red hair which went so well with her green eyes and pale skin. There was a sardonic twist to his mouth. Perhaps he could tell that it wasn't her real colour, that it went with everything else that was new about her. She'd had braces on her teeth then, eight years ago. Now her teeth were beautiful, different, perfectly aligned. Her generous dark eyebrows had been tamed to a sophisticated arch. Her voice was different too. She had taken acting lessons, including voice projection and modulation, had learned how to convey or hide emotion. For a time, a desire to act had vied with her conviction that she wanted to be a doctor.

'What was her name?' she added, not letting her smile slip, even though it was making her jaw ache.

'Patricia Ranley...if that was her real name,' he said softly, frowning down at her. 'Somehow I doubt it. I met her here at this clinic. We, the staff, called her Tricia for short.' Up close he towered over her, his eyes searching hers. He was as attractive as ever...more so.

'How come you remember her name?'

'She somehow stuck in my mind,' he said slowly, standing close to her as others milled around.

'You met her in your youth? And you must be all of thirty,' Laetitia quipped, resisting the urge to step back from such close proximity which she found unaccountably disturbing, forcing herself to laugh as she looked into those familiar, intelligent, grey-blue eyes which, she knew, could be warm with a rare kindness and understanding.

'Thirty-three, actually,' he said. The hand that held hers was dry and firm, while she felt that hers must be clammy with sudden nervous tension.

'And what did she do that she stuck in your mind?' she asked, withdrawing her hand. 'We certainly get a lot of interesting and unusual cases here.'

'I took her home,' he said. 'I didn't often do that. Well...to my sister's place, in actual fact.'

'Like a stray cat!' she said.

'You could say that,' he said, with a shrug and a wry smile.

'I'm Laetitia Lane,' she said. 'Titia for short.'

'Then you're married,' he murmured, almost absently,

as he stared at her, as though that was not what he had intended to say. A slight frown puckered his brows.

'No,' she said, 'that's my name. I'm not Patricia... whatever. I'm Laetitia Lane—Dr Lane, that is.' She mimicked his introduction, smiling, inviting him to smile with her. 'Which reminds me that I'm here to work, as I suppose you are. Have you had breakfast yet?'

'No.' He was still frowning, looking at her intently, her attempt to deflect his attention not working. The last of the first influx of their early morning clients milled around them, jostling them politely as they stood together.

'And have you received any sort of orientation to the clinic? If not, I guess I could spare you five minutes, if you like,' she said brightly. 'I know you've been here before...'

The smile she gave him was not reflected on his face.

'Those eyes...' he murmured. 'I could have sworn...'

Laetitia raised her beautifully arched eyebrows at him. Then he drew back from her. 'No, I guess I'm wrong,' he said.

'Looks like it,' she said.

'I would appreciate those five minutes. Thanks,' he said, more formally. 'Maybe that's all I need.'

'You...um...you're going to be working here regularly? No one told me we were getting a new doctor,' she said, struggling for composure. It was as though the intervening years were crumbling away...

'I'm just here for one day a week this time, although I may do more if I have free time from the hospital. Otherwise, I work at University Hospital, in the internal medicine department. Just started there recently. I used to work here in the clinic when it wasn't quite so organized. It had just got started then, eight years ago. Those were the pioneer days,' he explained, as they stood rather awkwardly together in the capacious side hall of the church which housed the clinic and drop-in centre. 'I asked for time out to do this. I can more or less organize my own time.'

'Really? That must have been interesting, being here in the pioneer days, as you put it,' she said, pretending she didn't know the previous circumstances of his work at the clinic. 'You must tell me about it some time.'

She busied herself, securing the heavy door to a brass hook attached to the wall so that it stayed open. 'I'm based at University Hospital, too—in Emergency Medicine. I'm doing an elective for three months in this clinic, part time, as part of my training, since it's emergency work of sorts.'

'You're a resident-in-training, then?' he said.

'Yes. I do three days a week here, sometimes a weekend, too, then two days at the hospital. I started here in mid-July.' That had been all of three weeks ago. In many ways it felt like she had been there for a very long time…memories of her own past at St Barnabas's church impinging on her recent experience. Just when she thought she was so *together*, as though none of that mattered any more, here it was, coming back to haunt her in the shape of Dr Grant Saxby.

'Sounds like a good arrangement,' he commented, still looking at her intently, at her every gesture, appearing to miss nothing. His voice was deep, attractive, just as she remembered it. 'Sounds as though you like it, too.'

Nervously, Titia stroked errant strands of hair from her forehead. 'Oh, I do! I love it. A lot of people who come here hate hospitals, won't go to one if they can possibly avoid it. It's partly because they get treated rudely there sometimes because they're street people. I suppose you could say that we take up the slack from the hospital emergency department.' Laetitia found herself chatting quickly, to hide her nervousness and a swift, renewed attraction. 'But, um, you must know all that...'

'I do know,' he said quietly. 'This place certainly fills a big gap in the medical services. I can appreciate why they would want to come here, not least because they often have to wait for hours to get seen in a hospital these days, with all the budget cuts.'

'Are you...working voluntarily?' she asked.

'Yes.'

'I'm getting paid myself, of course—' she felt the need to explain further '—but only because it's considered part of my training.' God knew, she herself had reason to be grateful to the volunteer doctors and medical students, as well as the rather poorly paid registered nurses, who had staffed the clinic eight years ago. 'We also have four dentists who volunteer their time and expertise. They don't come here, though, unless called in.'

'That's great,' he said.

Turning towards the few steps that led down to the passage to the Eating Place in the complex of rooms that made up the church building, Titia hoped to bring this particular interaction to an end. 'Shall we get coffee, Dr Saxby? I'm dying for one myself. You'll notice the difference, I expect...the coffee's really great!'

'Mmm. Call me Grant,' he said, as they walked.

'I'm Titia, if you like,' she volunteered, noting that his expression was thoughtful. She was very aware of him moving slowly by her side as they brought up the rear of the group of people moving to the Eating Place. So much for water under the bridge, she thought ruefully.

'I think I do like,' he said. Their voices were muted by the general chatter of conversation around them.

'This is a pretty informal place. A lot of my patients call me Tishy.'

'You're really an MD?' he queried. 'You look so young.'

'I'm an MD,' she confirmed, keeping it light. 'I did my training right here at the University of Gresham and at University Hospital, right here in good old Ontario, Canada. I want to be a trauma doctor—at least, that's my goal for now. I know that's the track for burn-out, if you're not very careful.'

'Mmm. That's really great!' he said, looking at her sideways as they walked. 'Especially being able to do a stint at a clinic like this.'

There was a still watchfulness about him, she thought, as though he could not figure her out, but was having a good try. 'Yes, I think so,' she enthused. 'It's wonderful experience. I see a bit of everything here.' She talked quickly to hide the way he was affecting her, hoping that none of it was showing on her face. She could tell—or thought she could—that he was not entirely convinced that she was not Patricia Ranley. Once, in another life, it seemed, she had had that teenage crush on him...

'So you're not married?' he asked quietly, persistently, a tinge of disbelief in his voice. 'And you're not Patricia Ranley? Titia and Tricia are very much the same.'

'I can't help that,' she said lightly, 'and it's no to both your questions. Not divorced either. I'm very much a career woman. Satisfied, Dr Sa— er, Grant?' How easy it was to lie sometimes, she thought, when you wanted to keep a lid on the past. Yet she did not like telling lies to this man; the deeper you got in, the more difficult it was to get out of any subterfuge.

'I'll have to be, won't I?' he said, something like subtle

sarcasm in his voice so that Titia's womanly antennae were instantly alerted.

Her intuition told her that this attractive man had, perhaps, a certain axe to grind where women were concerned. Crossed in love, perhaps? she speculated, feeling his attraction envelop her like a cloak...an unwanted attraction. At this time in her life she had enough on her plate with her job, without getting lured by her own emotions into an entanglement. So far in her career she had managed to keep relationships on a casual level. Again, her instinct warned her that this man could be trouble. There was an intensity about him, coupled with a barely disguised, quiet bitterness, if she was not mistaken. Better to keep him in the dark while they had to work together.

'What about your marital status since we're on the subject?' she said cheekily, diverting him away from herself. 'And anything else of an intimate nature that you might want to tell me, since you're so curious about me. After all, we might be thrown together for quite some time, and it's better to get a handle on someone early, isn't it?'

This time he relaxed, giving her a smile that did very positive things to her—as it had done all those years ago in her young life when she had been sweet sixteen, confused, unhappy, bereft, and so many other things, too.

'No, I'm not married,' he volunteered, after a moment's hesitation. Again that slightly bitter expression passed fleetingly over his face. 'Not divorced either. There was someone...that's finished, in every sense of the word.'

'I...don't mean to be inquisitive.' There had been something in his tone that made her want to apologize.

'No? Now I just have three or four casual girlfriends. Safety in numbers.'

'Oh!' she said, raising her eyebrows, more affected by his reply than she cared to let on. Grant Saxby as a mature man was somehow much more disturbing than he had been as a somewhat idealistic medical student eight years ago. So there had been something, or someone, upsetting in his background...and she didn't think it had been her. 'Three or four! Wow! Normal, at least, as well as in great demand. Hmm?'

He laughed, finally. She let out an inward sigh of relief. 'I'm not sure I know what normal is any more,' he said.

I do, she found herself thinking, as though the words were being articulated very clearly in her head. When I met you at sixteen, you seemed the only normal, sane person in a sea of madness.

Why didn't she just tell him who she was now, say how wonderful it was to see him? She held back, needing time to think. Rejection was something she didn't want from him—especially from him. After all, they had to work together. Work for her had always been a joy, a calming refuge, not least because she was good at her job.

When she had known him before her hair had been dyed black, with an over-sheen of dark blue that she had put on with a spray, which had been the fashion then. Changing one's hair colour had been a sign of asserting one's individuality, one's emerging identity, separate from parents, teachers, school rules. In those days she had worn thick eye make-up—purple shadow on the lids and several layers of thick black mascara which had made her look as though she had spiders' webs around her eyes. Only the eyes themselves were the same, a pale, clear green...those she could not disguise.

And it was these eyes that Dr Saxby was repeatedly

looking at now, highlighted as they were by the contrasting copper-red dye on her shining hair which tumbled in artful disarray around her face to just above her shoulders. It disguised her own light brown colour, which she had never liked.

'How come I've never seen you before in the hospital?' he said. 'I'm relatively new there, but we should have bumped into each other at least once.'

'It's a big place,' she said, shrugging, 'and the emergency department's a real madhouse. You must have been in there.'

'A few times,' he said.

'I'm usually tucked away somewhere in one of the ER operating rooms, stitching up someone, intubating them, putting in a chest tube here and there, washing out a few stomachs from overdoses, gunshot wounds, stab sounds. You name it, we get it. I'm not standing around at the front desk, trying to look glamorous, you know,' she said.

'Sounds as though you love it.' He smiled.

'I do,' she said, as they entered the eating area. 'Now I'm ready for that coffee.'

They were hailed immediately. 'Hey, come and get some coffee, Doc,' Dodge called to her from the other side of the large room that was the Eating Place. He stood next to one of the four coffee-urns that gave out a continuous supply of coffee throughout the day. It was here that volunteers prepared, cooked and served food.

Glad of the diversion, Titia walked toward him, weaving through the swelling crowd of hungry regulars. The hum of conversation was loud. 'I love coming in here,' Titia enthused to Grant Saxby, 'I love to see all these hungry people getting good food.'

'Ain't you gonna introduce me to the new doc?' Dodge

said as they came close. The man with the battered face had two mugs of coffee ready for them.

'Dodge,' she said, 'this is Dr Grant Saxby. Grant, this is Dodge.'

'Pleased-to-meecha,' Dodge slurred in his usual way, smiling, showing a mouthful of gray, rotting teeth. 'Dodge…Dodger…that's me. The artful dodger…see?'

'Yes.' Grant Saxby shook his head. 'I can see how that name could be very useful. I used to work here, you know, when I was an intern and a medical student. Did quite a long stint as a volunteer. I don't know how I had the energy, actually, when I think of all the other stuff I had to do at the hospital, Gresham General, where I interned.'

While Titia added cream and sugar to her coffee and helped herself to a giant-sized blueberry muffin, the two men chatted.

'That was before my time here. I'm from Nova Scotia, although I've been in Ontario a few years,' Dodge said, surprising Titia. Generally, he gave out as little personal information as possible, although in other ways he was very open.

She bit into the delicious muffin—one of several dozen donated free every morning by a local bakery—and listened to the two men talking. Soon, after this brief interlude for refreshment, they would start work, attending to the needs of those who had nowhere else to turn for medical help and those who shunned hospitals for various reasons. As she had told Grant Saxby, she loved the work, as though making up for the help she herself had received.

Titia found her mind wandering unerringly to the past, to things she had managed not to think about for a long time. Disturbingly, there was a sneaking feeling now that one of the reasons she worked so hard, focused on her career, was to keep any lingering thoughts of the past at bay.

When she had known Grant Saxby before, she had lied about her name because she had been so ashamed, among other things, of the fact that she had run away from home after her father's death, that she had been living on the street, either sleeping rough or in hostels. She had felt like a fraud, too, because she came from a comfortable home where she had always felt loved…until then. Even then she had known that things were different for a lot of young people of her age. During those two months on the street, a time that had felt more like two years, she had seen what it was like for those who were really un-loved, unwanted, and she had felt ashamed, as though she were somehow slumming for effect, to see what it was like. Maybe, in a way, she had been…

He, Grant, had said 'hey' to her then as well to get her attention. But he hadn't called her 'lady' then. No, he had called her 'little one'…

It had not been summertime then, the ideal time to sleep out if one had run away from home. It had been October, when the leaves had been falling off the trees and the temperature dropping at night. Cold, hungry and very frightened, yet determined not to give in and go home to her mother, she had gone into the church of St Barnabas one night. Someone had told her about the newly founded Open Door Clinic and drop-in centre, where you could get food and where you could some-times sleep if you had nowhere to go.

Crouching down, weeping, in one of the pews in the cavernous main body of the church, she had been found by Dr. Saxby.

'Hey…hey, little one. What is it? What's the matter, eh?' he had said.

When she had looked up slowly, peering at him through her wet, cobwebby eyelashes, he had been sitting next to her in the pew, one arm flung over the back of it as though he needed the support.

Although he had looked tired—it had been late in the evening—he had also looked not a great deal older than she had, almost boyish, with his slightly grubby white lab coat over jeans and a sweatshirt, his hair tousled as though he had not brushed it for several days. There had been a stethoscope stuffed into the breast pocket of his lab coat, and an identification badge with his photograph on it.

Knowing that her black mascara must be running in streaks down her face, making her look like a creature made up for a Halloween scare, she had looked at him warily, yet with relief, waiting for him to say something else.

'I'm one of the medicos here,' he said, 'a volunteer. My name's Grant. I heard you crying.'

His voice was gentle as he concentrated his attention on her. What she liked about him then was that he didn't come on like a professional helper, like a lot of people did when they were dealing with girls of her age, as if they were very conscious of doing good, that you were a 'case' to them. Neither was he patronizing.

Taking a packet of paper tissues out of his pocket, he offered them to her. 'Here, blow your nose. You can tell me about it if you want to. I'm here to help.'

After a few minutes of hesitation she had blurted it all out to him, about the grief and confusion that never left her for one moment. There in the dimly lit church where they were alone, with only muted traffic noises as a diversion, it was like a confessional, offering solace.

She told him how, only a short while previously, she had been a schoolgirl, starting a new academic year at her high school, with no worries in the world other than the usual ones which now seemed so petty that they were not worth considering. Then on one beautiful autumn day her mother had come to the school to pick her up by car, and her life had changed for ever.

'It's amazing,' she whispered to him in the quiet church, 'how one moment everything's great—you're happy—and then a minute or two later everything's changed... Nothing will ever be the same.'

'I know,' Grant said. 'Go on.'

'My mum told me that my dad had been in a car accident, that he was in the intensive care unit of University Hospital in a coma, with severe head injuries. It wasn't his fault, the accident. He...he'd been making a left turn at an intersection...someone ran a red light and smashed right into him.' Tears ran freely down her face as she spoke.

'Take it easy,' Grant said. 'Just take your time.'

'She...my mum...said that we should go to the hospital because...because he might not live very long.'

When she broke into sobs, remembering the awful poignancy and numbness of that scene in the car with her mother, and then later in the hospital, Grant put an arm around her shoulders and she rested her head against him.

'You're doing great,' he encouraged. 'You'll feel better when you've told me about it.'

'When we got to the hospital, my dad didn't know we were there... He never came out of the coma, you see, even though we were there for most of the time over the next three days,' she said. 'Then…he died…on the evening of the third day.'

There were long moments of silence while she leaned against him, composed herself as best she could.

'How come you happen to be here, in this church?' Grant said, at last, gently, with no hint of judgement or impersonal curiosity in his tone. 'Do you want to tell me about that?'

It was more difficult to explain how her mother had gone a little crazy after the accident, had taken up with a man who had known the family slightly—an unsuitable man. She had done it with unseemly haste, almost as though she had been sleep-walking, as though she hadn't really known what she'd been doing.

'He must have thought that my mother was a rich widow…that he could talk her into marrying him. He was in financial trouble, you see. I found that out later.'

Slowly, stiltedly, thinking it all through carefully as she spoke, she told Grant Saxby about the man, Terry, who had talked her mother into letting him come to live with her, how he had just gone through a divorce, how his wife had gained custody of their four young children. Telling it all to a stranger, in the peaceful atmosphere of the church, made certain things clearer to her.

'I…I felt as though I didn't really know my mother. She was like a stranger then,' she whispered.

'Sometimes it takes people that way,' Grant said. 'It's not unusual, believe me. It's sort of an attempt to put back the clock, to pretend that everything's normal…with another person, who might not be at all like the person they're replacing. Yet they try to delude themselves that it really is the same person. It's that "on the rebound" thing—only in a more extreme form, by the sound of it.'

'That's it,' she said vehemently. 'I was so frightened. I still am.'

'I can imagine it.'

'And he's such a...slimy sort of person, an opportunist, I guess you could call him,' she finished up. 'I guess he plays on my mother's own needs, and her willingness to be sympathetic to other people when she's suffering so much herself.'

'I think that's quite common, too,' he said gently. 'It takes the focus away from your own pain.'

'Yes...I think that's it,' she said, beginning to feel that at last she was sharing her awful burden.

'So you ran away?' Grant said.

'Yes. It was partly that I could see what was happening, how he was taking advantage of my mother, and it was partly that he hit me—just once. I thought that if I went...it would shock her into seeing what she was doing. She had sort of...created an illusion.'

She concentrated hard on what she had felt, living at home with her mother and the other man. Amazingly, it was easy to talk to this young doctor; she found the sentences tumbling out, as though in the time she had been away from home the explanation had formed itself more coherently in her mind, just waiting for the right moment to be brought out. 'Does that make sense?' she added.

'Yes, perfect sense,' he said, nodding in commiseration.

'I...I only just sorted it out completely,' she confessed hesitantly, 'because of what you said.'

'Something more specific—him hitting you—must have led up to you running away,' Grant said, prompting gently.

'Yes,' she whispered. 'I confronted Terry one evening when my mother was late getting home from work. I...I accused him of being a slime-bag. That's when he hit me…slapped me hard around the face.'

Grant's arm tightened around her shoulders as she struggled to go on, to tell her story.

'It's all right now, take it easy. So you decided to leave then and there?' he prompted.

'Yes…'

'Doc! Hey, Doc! Are you with us, or what?'

The voice of Dodge brought Titia back quickly, with a peculiar mental jolt, to the here and now. The scene from her past had been so vivid that, to her surprise, she realized she had automatically chomped her way through the blueberry muffin and had drunk almost all the mug of coffee, without being aware of doing so.

'It's "what", I guess.' She laughed. 'Sorry. Just ruminating on all that I have to get through today.'

An odd feeling of happiness came over her as she looked at her two companions. The things she had been thinking about made her realize that since that time her life had got steadily better. Meeting Grant Saxby that first time had been the start of her return to a calmness, a common-sense reality, about her loss. Yet she had built fantasies around him at the age of sixteen, fantasies that belonged to extreme youth. Then a more urgent reality had hit, the need to get an education, to learn how to earn a living, get a career…

'Well, back to the grind,' she said in a businesslike way. 'I'll show you around, Dr Saxby.'

'You gonna cut my toenails today, Tishy?' Dodge said to her as she prepared to leave the Eating Place. 'I sure like the way you do it.'

Grant laughed, looking at her, it seemed, with a new interest, raising his eyebrows, while she grinned, her colour rising.

'Well, sure!' she said. 'Unless Esther beats me to it.
I'm sure there's a lot of competition to cut your toenails,
Dodge.'

'You can fight it out between you,' Dodge said.

'Esther's one of the registered nurses here,' Titia explained as she and Grant left the room. 'She'll be in the
clinic, I expect, so I'll introduce you.'

'Great!'

'We spend quite a lot of time soaking our patients'
feet, cutting toenails, treating athlete's foot, getting rid of
corns, and so on. In fact, we have some volunteers here
who come in just to deal with all the foot problems. Our
patients are so grateful just to sit with their feet in a bowl
of warm, soapy water.'

'Yeah, I can imagine. I remember that,' he said. 'Looking at feet and teeth is very important.'

'We give them clean socks, if we have any on hand,
and offer them other shoes that we get donated,' she
added.

'I'm looking forward to it,' he said, grinning. 'Makes
a change.'

The two doctors walked side by side back along the
corridor to the side entrance hall, then they turned right
off the hall to go to a suite of four rooms, plus a tiny
office and supply room, that made up the Open Door
medical and nursing clinic. Two of the larger rooms were
divided up into examination cubicles behind curtains, one
room for men and one for women, with six cubicles each.
The waiting area was in a corridor. Titia tried hard not
to let Grant Saxby suspect how much his sudden appearance had unsettled her, especially how surprised she
was by the fact. No one had told her that a new doctor
was starting today.

'It looks a lot better equipped than when I was last

here,' Grant commented, walking easily beside her, looking cool in his lightweight clothes which were so suitable
for the promised sweltering day ahead.

Titia was about to agree, then bit back the retort. At
this point she did not want him to get even a hint that
she had seen the clinic all those years ago to confirm his
suspicions. After all, she had a professional and social
position to maintain now. None of her colleagues knew
that she had spent two months living on the street in her
youth. Even though she trusted Grant implicitly, she
didn't want it to get out somehow. Some people were
prejudiced that way.

After she had shown Grant the rooms, the two others
being used for treatments of a more serious nature, such
as the suturing of wounds, they met the nurse coming out
of the office.

'Oh, hi!' she said. 'You must be Dr Saxby. I'm Esther
Stanfield. Old-fashioned name, old-fashioned girl. I don't
mind admitting it.' They shook hands. The nurse, in her
early forties, had that slightly weathered look of one who
had worked very hard all her professional life. She was
a good nurse—intelligent, shrewd and compassionate,
Titia thought, well suited to this type of work, able to
turn her hand to anything that might come through the
doors of the clinic.

'Good to meet you, Esther,' Grant smiled warmly. 'My
colleague here…' he glanced at Titia '…didn't know you
were getting a new doctor. I guess it was all arranged in
a hurry.'

'Sorry about that, Dr Lane,' the nurse said. 'I didn't
know myself until this weekend, when the director of
staff told me over the phone that she'd found someone
at short notice to cover the holiday period and beyond.
There's a high burn-out rate here, for both doctors and

nurses. The main thing that gets to you is the frustration that comes from not being able to do enough.'

'Yes,' Grant commiserated.

'You know what it's like to treat someone here for flu or pneumonia on a cold night,' the nurse went on, 'and then have to put them out on the street if there's nowhere for them to sleep here. We do let them sleep in the pews if our other rooms are full, but we're not supposed to because of fire regulations.'

'I'm afraid I do know,' Grant said soberly. 'When I was here before, we used to let them sleep in the church, too.'

'Yes. We live in fear that someone will light up a cigarette in there and burn the place down,' Esther said, with a wry laugh.

'But you've got some permanent beds here now?' Grant said.

'Yes. We've set up an overnight sleeping place,' Esther said, 'and we nurses take it in turns to do a night shift to take care of the ones who are really sick. But it's unofficial—we're not supposed to have anyone overnight. The church minister knows, of course. He's with us all the way. So far we've only got twelve beds. That's all we can cope with for now.'

'Hmm,' Grant said. 'Maybe that's something that can be changed—the unofficial bit. I suppose it has something to do with fire regulations, as you say.'

'You're welcome to try, Dr Saxby,' Esther said, with a weary air. 'Dr Lane here has been working on it for several weeks, without letting the authorities know that we're already doing it in a small way. It's like smashing your head against the proverbial brick wall.'

'I'm going to make a start with my patients,' Titia said, having spotted some of her regulars sitting down in the waiting area in the corridor. 'I have a feeling it's going to be one of those days. With this heat, we get a lot of dehydrated people here.' She had addressed herself to Grant.

'Sure, you go ahead,' he said, 'otherwise I might find myself competing with you to cut that guy's toenails.'

The slow grin he gave her made her almost give herself away, and she laughed at the mental image he evoked of the two of them fighting over the privilege of dealing with Dodge's gnarled feet. Foot problems were the bane of the street people, having to walk a lot and frequently being moved on by the police.

'Oh, there's plenty of that sort of competition here,' Esther chipped in. 'Competition *not* to do certain things! Right, Dr Lane?'

'Right.'

'Ever deloused anybody, Dr Saxby?' the nurse said.

'Not yet. That's something I'm looking forward to. Make sure you call me when there's a case, eh?' He smiled, standing casually with his hands in his trouser pockets, as though he were eagerly waiting to be confronted with a case of body or head lice.

'I intend to,' Esther said crisply. 'We get scabies, too, and fleas. You name it, we get it.'

'That's exactly what I went to medical school for,' Laetitia joked. 'Anyway, excuse me, Dr Saxby, I'm sure Esther will show you the drug cupboard and the other medical supplies.'

'Thanks, Dr Lane,' he said. 'I won't hesitate to call on you if I need to.'

Making her escape, Titia hurried to the corner area of the women's examination room which was her own private space. The remainder of the room was divided up into the six curtained areas, each with its own examination table. Here, in her corner, secluded behind a wooden folding privacy screen, she had her own desk, chair, filing cabinet and bookshelves. It was a little oasis in a place where there was little real privacy for anyone. They did their best with the curtains and screens.

Behind her screen she sank into the wooden upright chair, put her elbows on the desk and her head in her hands. Ghosts from the past had come back to haunt her without warning. At that moment she knew that she was not entirely free of their influence, or the girlish emotion she had felt for Grant Saxby.

With that came the apprehension that he, the mature Grant Saxby, would not want to get to know her as a woman, a woman who had been a runaway girl—that was what he had called her when she had refused at first to give her name. And she found that part of her wanted him to get to know her while the other part shied away from him, warned her to keep her distance at all costs.

Even if she got up the courage to tell him who she was, it was highly likely that he would reject her as a woman, if not as a colleague. No, he would accept her as a colleague, she decided as an afterthought. He was not a snob, not the rejecting sort. But it was one thing to help a girl in desperate need, and quite another to accept her later on in life. He had seemed friendly enough, almost as though he was disappointed that she had not admitted to being Patricia Ranley. But fantasy was not the same as reality. Would he care for her as a mature woman? She thought perhaps not. Obsessively she mulled it over. She could not risk exposure at the moment.

She had moved on from all that and had come to terms with her past...if only he would let her forget...

CHAPTER TWO

THE waiting area in the hallway was filling up. Titia stood in the doorway of the women's treatment room and surveyed the group of people there. Grant had taken up a position in the men's treatment room, while Esther would work out of the office, transferring her patients to a cubicle in either of the other rooms as necessary. It was a simple system which worked well in the space that they had available.

'Who's first?' she called out.

'I am.' Rita, one of her regulars, who was a diabetic, got up wearily from her chair, humping a large, grubby, blue nylon holdall in which she carried her immediate worldly goods.

A middle-aged woman, looking older than her years, she was unhealthily thin, pale, with sparse light brown hair which had strands of grey in it. Titia knew her story well. Widowed, fallen upon hard times, she had lost her job about nine months ago and had since found it impossible to pay rent. After staying with friends for short periods, she had found herself homeless. Nonetheless, her sense of humour seldom left her.

'I don't feel too good these days,' she said to Titia, once they were inside the other room. 'I'm getting terrible headaches, I get the shakes…it's this diabetes. I can't afford to buy them expensive blood-sugar test kits.'

'Lie down on the couch, Rita,' Titia said, swishing aside the curtains of a cubicle. 'I'll take a look at you, do your blood pressure and a blood-sugar test.'

'I know you said I should come here to get the blood-sugar test done so that I don't have to buy the kit, but I'm not always in this part of town, you know,' Rita explained, heaving herself up onto the couch. 'I'm so weary...so, so weary.'

'You've been to visit your daughter?'

'Yes. She lives out in the west end. I expect I told you that. It's a long way.' Rita talked while she removed her top clothing so that Titia could listen to her heart with the stethoscope, a simple procedure that always seemed to reassure patients.

'My daughter's always saying to me, ''come and live with me, Mum, I worry about you so much when you don't have a place of your own.'' But, you know, Dr Lane, I don't like her husband. I don't like the way he looks at me, like I was the scum of the earth or something because I don't have a place. He scares me. If she was on her own, I'd be there like a shot, believe me! I don't say that to her, of course, but I'm sure she knows how I feel. Course, he's not her real husband...they never married...'

Carefully Titia placed the tip of her stethoscope on Rita's chest, moving it from place to place. The heartbeat was rapid and thready. Rita was not a healthy woman—she needed to be in a hospital for a complete work-up, to have her diabetes stabilized.

As it was, she injected herself with insulin whenever she felt that she needed it, having learned how to recognize the symptoms of her disease—of too much sugar in her bloodstream, or not enough.

She was supposed to balance the insulin with her meals, to test her blood sugar with a simple finger-prick test, but quite often she did not bother to be accurate. A lot of the time she just went by her symptoms. And the blood-test kits were expensive, although she could get them free from the clinic when she was in the area. Diabetes was a complex disease, producing an array of acute and chronic effects.

Without hurrying, Titia took Rita's blood pressure, then pricked a finger to do a quick and easy blood-sugar test. She looked into Rita's eyes with an ophthalmoscope, searching for the beginnings of the eye disease that was common in diabetics, which could lead to blindness over time. All the time Rita talked, letting out all the angst that had accumulated in her life since she had last come to the clinic.

'Let me have a look at your feet,' Titia said. 'Any problems there?' Gangrene of the feet, resulting from poor peripheral circulation, was common in diabetics, particularly gangrene of the big toe.

'Not since I had the ingrowing toenails operated on,' Rita said. 'I have you to thank for that, Doc. That was one of the best moves I ever made.'

'Before you go, we'll give you a foot treatment as usual, cut your nails and so on.'

'I'm looking forward to that,' Rita said, sighing at the thought of having her aching feet in a bowl of frothy, scented water.

A little later, as she jotted down the findings from the physical examination in Rita's file, Titia made up her mind about something.

'We have another doctor here today, Rita. His name's Dr Saxby,' she said. 'You probably saw him in the Eating Place?'

'Yeah. Nice-looking guy.' Rita chuckled. 'Wouldn't mind getting my hands on him for a night or two.'

'I expect a few other people would second that.' Titia laughed.

'You're right there.' Rita broke into a wheezy laugh. 'Chance would be a fine thing, eh?'

'Yes,' Titia agreed thoughtfully, feeling her cheeks flush slightly. 'Anyway, I want to ask him to take a look at you, Rita, because he works in the internal medicine department at University Hospital. Would you consider coming into hospital for a few days for a comprehensive check-up? He could get you admitted there, have your diabetes stabilized, then we could take a chest X-ray, a pap smear, a mammogram, some blood work—the works, in fact.'

'Sounds great to me. I wouldn't say no to a few days of free food and a proper bed to sleep in,' Rita said.

'There's nothing much to worry about,' Titia assured her. 'It's just that from time to time you need to have a few tests that we can't easily do here.'

'Right. As I said, I do feel somewhat lousy right now. I've lost weight, I don't get enough decent food. That's a big part of the problem.'

'We're still working on getting you an apartment in the local public housing place. Are you still interested?' Titia said.

'I sure am,' Rita said. 'I'm pretty tired of toting that bag, I can tell you. I've got stuff at my daughter's, too. Mind you, I don't tell that "husband" of hers. He'd throw it all out!'

'I call them every week at the housing place. I don't let them forget you,' Titia said, knowing that Rita needed something to hope for. 'With luck, we'll have you in there before the winter.'

'Pigs might fly,' Rita said resignedly, 'but I'll keep praying. I appreciate that you're rooting for me, Dr Lane.'

When she had written her preliminary notes of her

findings, Titia went in search of Grant. Rita was a casualty of circumstances beyond her own control—she had become ill, unable to work regularly, even before she lost her job. It was a very familiar story.

There was a certain delight in knowing that Grant was there, Titia thought, that he was her colleague and that she could call upon him for a consultation. There was a momentary odd feeling that maybe she had just conjured him up out of her imagination. After all, she didn't have any serious men friends, only casual ones. Not that she didn't have offers, but somehow they didn't seem quite right for anything other than very casual liaisons. Up to now, that was the way she had wanted it. Somehow the presence of Grant Saxby was beginning to upset her assumptions of complete self-sufficiency.

'Looking for me?' Grant glanced up from his desk, which was identical to her own, behind a similar screen in a corner of the men's examination room, where he was bending over to write in a file. 'Or are you just checking up on me to see that I can cope?'

Strands of dark hair flopped across his forehead, making him look deceptively young. Only close up could one see the lines of tiredness around the eyes that hinted at the strain of his profession. Those eyes narrowed as he looked at her perceptively so that Titia sensed that he knew darn well who she was.

'Well…' she said, deliberately leaving the word hanging. In spite of her internal resistance, a feeling of being cared for, a remembered warmth, came over her like a physical thing from long ago. That was how he had made her feel then. It was so strange. There had been a genuineness about him—it was still there, a part of him. Yet there was something different…a watchfulness, a carefulness, which she sensed rather than saw in him now.

'No lice yet,' he quipped, raising his eyebrows at her and running a hand through his own thick hair which was so obviously clean and shining with health.

'They come in at about four o'clock,' she said, 'just when you're ready to go home.'

'I'll deal with the first one,' he said, 'if you'll promise to come out for a drink with me afterwards.'

'That's blackmail.' She laughed.

'Yeah. I've found it works better than anything.'

'Oh? That's a bit cynical, Dr Saxby.'

'Occupational hazard,' he said.

'Esther usually deals with those cases, unless there's a run on head lice,' she said.

'We have to keep our hands in, too,' he persisted. 'Perhaps you'll come out for a drink with me, head lice or no?' he said, straightening up to his full height.

'Sure,' she said coolly. 'That would be nice.'

'Time and place to be decided by me?'

Titia shrugged, fighting the attraction. Things were going too quickly for her. 'Actually, if you're free now,' she said, avoiding the question, 'would you mind doing a consult on a regular patient of mine? She's a diabetic.' In a few words, she outlined Rita's problems and her need to be admitted to a hospital for a few days for tests.

'Sure, I'll see her,' he agreed. 'Just give me a couple of minutes to finish these notes. And you didn't answer my question, Dr Lane.'

'I need time to think about that,' Titia said, pushing back her tumbled hair from her face, self-conscious suddenly, feeling unusually aware of her appearance. Maybe that had something to do with the fact that he was looking at her again, not as a colleague but as though she were an attractive woman. Usually at work she forgot her appearance, gave everything to her job, where not many activities made one feel attractive. She felt a slow heat invading her body, much to her annoyance.

'Hmm. Don't take too long, Titia.'

'I'll take as long as I please,' she murmured, so that his patient could not hear. 'And thanks for the consult.'

'My pleasure,' he said quietly.

'I thought that while she's in hospital,' Titia went on, with a rush, determined to get back to business, 'I might finally be able to get her into the local public housing project. I've been trying for weeks to get her in there, into an apartment. I've known Rita for quite a while because I used to work here some weekends before I was seconded to work during the week. I think she's getting pretty depressed from not having a place of her own.'

'Yes, her hospitalization might be the impetus to get her in,' Grant agreed. 'I know they have a waiting list, but they also have a priority list.'

'When they know she's in hospital and will have to be discharged literally onto the street,' Titia added, warming to her subject, 'maybe they'll be shamed into letting her have a place.'

'Hmm,' he said again. 'We can't count on it coming at the right time, though. Have they got any empty places?'

'Yes, I know for a fact that one may be coming up soon,' she said.

'Maybe I can help. We'll make it a joint effort. Anyway, I'll be with you in a moment.'

When Titia went out into the corridor, a loud voice hailed her from the small office. 'Hey, Tishy! Esther's got my feet!' It was Dodge, sitting in splendour in the office with his feet immersed in soapy, scented water in a large plastic bowl. His tattered jeans were rolled up to mid-calf level. As he luxuriated in a comfortable chair, he sipped a cup of coffee.

'Oh, shame!' Titia smiled as she leaned against the doorframe. It was evident that Dodge had already had a shower. His hair was wet and there was a strong smell of scented soap. Evidently he was wearing his second set of clothes, probably while his others were being washed in the launderette. In his way he was a fastidious man, at least where his clothes were concerned, hanging onto shreds of dignity.

'Aren't I the lucky one, eh?' Esther laughed.

'I envy you desperately.' Titia felt laughter bubbling up inside her, a sense of carefree happiness that she did not usually experience in quite such a degree in the clinic. That feeling undoubtedly had a lot to do with the unexpected presence of Grant Saxby.

'I've persuaded Dodge to see the dentist later on this morning, since the dentist's coming in to see someone else,' Esther informed Titia. 'We don't want gingivitis setting in, do we? Dodge doesn't look after his teeth the way he looks after his feet.'

'It's not as pleasurable,' Titia observed.

'Gingy…what?' Dodge said.

'Gingivitis,' Esther informed him. 'It's when you get gum disease because you don't look after your teeth. It can spread to the bones of your jaw and cause a real bad mess.'

'You trying to scare me, or what?' Dodge said.

'I'd be really pleased if I could scare you,' Esther added, sitting down on a low stool in front of Dodge's face. 'You don't want to go around huffing that bad breath over everyone, do you?'

'All right, all right, I give in,' he said. 'Nobody said anything about bad breath before, or that gingy thing.'

'They're being too polite.' Titia grinned.

'Sister Albertina's here,' Esther said, looking up at Titia. 'She'll do the feet for us today, from now on.'

'That's great!' Titia said. 'I've got Rita Cook who needs to have her feet done. I've got her on an examination couch right now. I'm getting Dr Saxby to do a consult.'

'I'll ask Sister Albertina to go there, then,' Esther said.

The nun, Sister Albertina, from a lay order that worked with disadvantaged people in the inner city of Gresham, came to the clinic several times a week as a volunteer to attend to feet, to wash them, give first aid and deal with any chronic problems.

'Funny, ain't it, that people who don't have anywhere to go have to walk a lot, have to keep moving? It's like they have to pretend they're going somewhere,' Dodge chipped in. 'Kind of ironic, ain't it?'

'There are many such ironies in this life, Dodge,' Esther said. 'We see more than our fair share of them here.'

'They're called layabouts.' Dodge chuckled, showing his awful teeth. 'But they don't do much laying about when you come to think about it. It's just that they have to do their laying about in public a lot of the time.'

'Some of them do quite a lot of laying about, Dodge,' Esther said.

'Not me,' Dodge said. 'I seem to spend all my time going from A to B to C, then back again.'

Titia left them to it and hurried back to Rita. The eyes of the people in the waiting area followed her, reminding her that they still had a lot of work to get through. Sister Albertina would weed out those who did not need to see a doctor or a nurse.

It did not take long for Grant to arrange for Rita to be

admitted in two days' time to hospital, even though it was not easy, in this time of budget cuts and waiting lists for beds, to find a space when you needed one. Rita clearly could not wait. For the two days of waiting she was invited to sleep at the clinic if she wanted to.

'Thanks,' Rita said. 'I'll do that. Then at least I'll be clean when I go into the hospital, won't I?'

'Yes,' Titia agreed, 'and we've got the hairdresser coming tomorrow so you can get your hair done, too.'

'This is my lucky day,' Rita said, gathering up her clothes and stuffing them into her nylon holdall. 'Have you got something I could wear, Dr Lane, while I throw my clothes in a washing machine?'

'Sure,' Titia said, pleased that her patient had not put up any resistance about going into hospital. In fact, she seemed resigned and relieved. 'Come back here when you've done that. Sister Albertina's coming to fix your feet in a few minutes.'

'Oh, great! I'll get one of the other girls to take my stuff out of the machine, then I'll grab myself a cup of the old cappuccino and be right back.'

The morning went by very quickly, with the staff working their way steadily through a variety of patients. Sister Albertina, a stout woman of indeterminate age with a serene, kind face, was a prominent presence in the clinic. In her white habit and flowing, old-fashioned headdress, she worked steadily and with purpose, dealing mainly with filthy, painful feet. With her gentle touch, soothing voice and quiet ways, she was like the archetypal angel of mercy. She had a sense of humour which kept the patients and staff smiling. Her favourite expression was, 'All this is enough to make you take up smoking in a big way.' They all suspected her of having a few illicit puffs behind the church during her coffee-breaks.

There were immigrants who did not speak English, where communication was through an innovative repertoire of sign language and smiles of encouragement from both sides. Some were illegal immigrants who had no desire to go to a hospital unless they really had to, for fear of being reported to the authorities. There was an endless array of interesting cases, a microcosm of the world. Many were young people who had left unbearable or impossible home situations. Titia's heart went out to them, these young ones who were little more than children and who were desperately trying to cope with a grown-up world not of their own making. So like her young self...

'I think we've earned a coffee-break at least, don't you, Dr Lane?' Grant came into her makeshift office, breaking into her thoughts, as she was filing her charts.

'Definitely,' she said, his presence making her tense.

'The waiting area's actually empty. I guess they've gone to eat,' he said, seeming to fill up the tiny space behind the screen. 'Shall we make our escape while we've got the chance?'

'Where to?' She looked at him over her shoulder. 'I could sure use a coffee. We could eat at the Eating Place, but it's nice to get away for a while.'

'Sure. Come on, I'll treat you. There's a little place over on the next street that I know well,' Grant said, shrugging out of his lab coat and leaving it on her chair. 'Esther has practically ordered us to get out for half an hour or so, then it's her turn.'

Titia took off her lab coat and flung it with his, an oddly intimate gesture. 'That's the best invitation I've heard in a long time,' she said, trying to hide the fact that she wasn't sure she was ready to lunch with him just yet. 'But I insist on paying for myself.'

'OK, independent lady.'

Titia could not help giving him a surreptitious appraising glance as he walked ahead of her. The thin linen of
his shirt clung to his muscled torso; she wondered what
his skin would feel like beneath it, and she imagined
herself running her fingertips lightly over his bare back.
Biting her lip, she dragged her eyes away from him. Perhaps she was suffering—the thought came to her unbid-
den, annoyingly—from all work and not much play.

Quickly she put on her sunglasses as they emerged.
The sun was fierce as they walked outside, striking her
bare arms and legs, a contrast to the relatively cool interior of the church. She wore a short, straight skirt of
linen and a sleeveless top in a pale cream colour that
accentuated the rich colour of her hair. From time to time
she felt Grant's eyes on her, assessing her. The thought
came to her that he might be thinking the same thoughts
about her that she had just been having about him.

They left the familiar street where the church was situated on a corner, to take a short cut through an alley to
the next street south. There were many of these alleys,
like a maze, in downtown Gresham. Titia felt a numbness
in her, a distancing, as though she were acting a part.
Maybe she was. It wasn't always easy to pin down your
own identity when so much of it was handed to you by
others. At last she thought she knew who she was, who
she wanted to be. At some point she would have to tell
him...

The little place on the next street proved to be a diner,
a small café for working men mostly, where the food was
good, cheap and unpretentious. The interior was air-
conditioned, cool. They took trays and went to the single
counter to order food.

'I'm going to have iced tea, a salad and Italian crusty

bread,' Titia said brightly as she eyed a chalked menu on a blackboard above the serving counter, hiding her lack of ease, going ahead of Grant. 'I'm starving, too.'

'A good choice for this heat,' he said, lining up behind her, joining the short queue of muscular individuals ahead of them who looked like a bevy of truck drivers, complete with tattoos over their bulging biceps. They turned to stare at Titia admiringly as she ordered her food so that she felt her face colouring, at the same time very physically aware of Grant close beside her.

'I'm not sure I'd want to come here by myself,' she murmured to him. 'Have you noticed that I'm the only woman in the place?'

'I had noticed,' he replied. 'With that hair, you're like a beacon to any male.'

'Oh?' she laughed. 'Is that the only reason?'

'No…' He was flirting with her and she found that she liked it, in spite of the underlying tension. In this world of raw, sweaty masculinity she felt like a fragile bird.

When they were seated at a table for two at the end of the single narrow room that made up the diner, shielded by a tall potted plant, Grant looked at her squarely across the mere two feet of the Formica-topped table between them. Under the table she felt his knee brush hers momentarily. She knew it was accidental, yet it sent a rush of heat through her, and something of her adolescent feelings for him as well. Maybe when she got to know him better she would find that he was different from her previous certainties.

'The girl I met at the clinic eight years ago, Patricia Ranley…' he was saying, breaking into her obsessive thoughts. 'I want to talk about her. Do you mind?'

'No. Why should I? Is that why you wanted to bring

me here? A captive audience?' she looked at him chal-
lengingly, trying to make light of it.

'Yes, partly. Some things gnaw at you for years. She
was one of them,' he said. 'I've seen many Patricia
Ranleys since then, but there was something about her...
She wasn't your typical runaway.'

'Please, go ahead, talk,' Titia said. Nonchalantly she
sipped the iced tea.

'She had just lost her father and had run away from
home because her mother had immediately taken up with
another man,' he said abruptly. 'We met in St Barnabas's
church late one evening. I tried to help her, I thought I
had helped her. I knew her for three weeks, then I never
saw her again.' The voice was quiet, his eyes boring into
hers.

'And...?' she said, her hands automatically picking up
the knife and fork. The persona she had developed over
the past few years stood her in good stead now as she
felt the challenge in his regard. Oddly, she could not tell
him, even now when she had the perfect opportunity, that
she was that girl. The words would not come.

What was it he had said to her all those years ago? It
came back to her. 'We're all multi-faceted,' he had said.
'If you don't like the identity that has been given to you
by the circumstances of your childhood, you pick a facet
of your personality that you *do* like. You develop that—
you become what *you* want to be. That's a way out for
you.'

'Yes,' she had said, grateful to him for offering her a
way out, for giving her permission, so to speak. She had
understood him perfectly. Fortunately for her she had always been good at school, had always worked hard there.
It had been that hard work which had enabled her to get
into medical school, to take the advice he had given.

'If you won't tell me your name,' he had said, 'I'll call you "runaway girl".'

'All right,' she had said, relieved. 'Maybe I'll tell you some time.'

Now, in the café, he was looking at her as though he had been waiting to get her in this situation where she was more or less trapped, yet he had been the one who had initiated the change in her from frightened, insecure schoolgirl to sophisticated professional, Laetitia Lane MD.

'You remind me so much of her. It's uncanny,' he said.

'Sorry,' she said.

'Oh, don't be sorry. It's time I came to terms with her,' he said. 'I guess I never quite forgave her for disappearing so abruptly from my life.'

'Without saying goodbye?'

'She said goodbye, in a note,' he said pensively. 'She wrote me a few words, thanking me. It turned out she lied about her name and where she lived.'

'Maybe she had reason to,' Titia said. She lifted the glass of iced tea to her mouth, aware that her lips were trembling as she took a small sip of the liquid.

'Perhaps,' he said. 'Then, on the other hand, maybe she lied about other things, too.'

'Why would she do that?' Titia said, trying to quell the indignation he was provoking in her, making her voice sharp. Maybe that was his intention.

Grant shrugged. 'Who knows? I was somewhat naïve in some things then, idealistic.'

'I…I'm sure she must have appreciated your concern.' Titia looked at her wristwatch. 'We've got less than fifteen minutes in which to finish this food.'

They finished the meal in silence, surrounded by the conversation of truck drivers. The streets were filled with lunchtime traffic, vehicles and pedestrians, when they emerged. Dodging traffic, they crossed the road to get to the alley, with Grant's hand on her arm. As they hurried along in the relative quiet of the alley, with tall, window-less buildings on either side, he kept his grip on her arm. Halfway along, between one street and the next, Grant suddenly entered a secluded doorway, a side service en-trance to a building, pulling her with him.

Titia found herself in a corner, with Grant's arm propped on the wall between her and the exit. With his other hand he took off her sunglasses and looked at her, his face only a few inches from hers. 'You're that girl, aren't you, Dr Laetitia Lane? No two women in the world could have eyes like that.'

Titia moistened her dry lips with the tip of her tongue, staring at him as though mesmerized, her eyes finally focusing on his very masculine mouth so close to her own, the well-shaped lips now compressed into an un-smiling line.

As Grant bent his head down to her, she drew in her breath sharply, the sound superimposed on the muted traffic noises from the street. His lips grazed her own for about three seconds, tantalizingly, his head blocking out the light.

'Why did you do that?' she gasped. 'We've known each other for, um, a little over four hours.'

'Have we?' he said, his expression veiled. 'It just hap-pened. I felt like it. Do you mind?'

'Well, I…'

'Do you mind?'

'No.' She drew in a deep breath. The truth was that she was so intensely aware of him that she felt she could scarcely breathe, her whole body tensed with expectation.

There was no way that he could not see her response, her darkened eyes.

'Instead of the three or four women that you've got, you want five or six? Hmm?' She murmured the words jokingly, trying to control an annoying tremor in her voice which, again, he could not fail to notice.

'Why not?' he said, his mouth twisted into that slightly sardonic smile she was beginning to get used to.

'That, again, sounds a bit cynical.'

'That's the voice of experience, is it?' he queried.

'Well…no,' she admitted.

'It's you, isn't it? You're my runaway girl?' he said again, not moving away from her or taking his eyes from her face, his propped arm keeping her prisoner.

'Yes…if you really must know,' she said, giving in. There was no point in keeping up the lie.

'Why didn't you say so right away?' he persisted.

'I don't want to open old wounds, to say the least,' Titia said with exasperation. 'There's no point in dwelling on the past. No one else knows about it, and I want to keep it that way.'

'I can keep a confidence,' he said.

'Good. Please keep to that,' she said, shifting her weight from one foot to the other restlessly. 'We must go now. We're going to be late and Esther will wonder what we're doing.' Somewhat shocked by her response to him, by the fact that this was happening at all, Titia strove for control, contradictory emotions forcing her to acknowledge that she liked being close to him. Such proximity reminded her of that other closeness with him in the past. Without too much trouble, for reasons of his own, he had made her confess.

'You're a pretty convincing liar,' he said, his voice

even, although there was a tenseness about him. There was a touch of admiration in his tone.

'Because I don't want to be reminded of it, by you or anyone else.' Titia ground out the words, anger and something like humiliation vying with emotions engendered by her reluctant attraction to him. She found herself very close to tears. 'I'm a different person now. Why are you going on and on about it, anyway?'

'I'm curious to know why you took off so abruptly then. Again, that's a common phenomenon in this business, but I was convinced at the time that you were different. Maybe I should have known better. Call it unfinished business. That has a way of nagging at you for a hell of a long time.'

'I was just a kid. Why are you so bothered?' she said, raising her voice.

'I cared...then,' he said.

When she stared at him, biting her lip, he stared back, an unreadable expression on his face. 'Now that I know,' he said at last, 'maybe we can forget about it.'

'Yes,' she said emphatically. 'As I said, the fewer people who know about it, the better. None of my colleagues know—and that's the way I want it to stay.'

'I don't like being lied to,' he said. 'I don't see the point. If you don't trust me...didn't trust me then...say so.'

'If you don't see the point,' she said, 'then I can't explain right now. It's not about trust. And I don't see why I should have to, anyway.' She straightened up, moving sideways. 'After today, Dr Saxby, maybe we should confine our interaction to work.'

For a long moment Grant looked at her. 'That's a pity,' he said, on a long sigh. The sardonic expression was back on his face. 'I was rather hoping for something more.'

She looked at him with narrowed eyes, unable to tell whether he was sincere or being sarcastic, goading her. Nevertheless she felt her cheeks flush with deep colour. 'That's the way I want it,' she said hotly, 'because I rather suspect that the "something more" would be on your terms. Am I right?'

'Maybe,' he said, noncommittally.

'You were such a nice guy, all those years ago,' Titia said, remembering. 'Something tells me you've changed a lot. Now, let's get out of here!'

They were ten minutes late when they got back to the clinic. Titia sought out Esther immediately. 'Sorry we're a bit late, Esther,' she apologized, hoping that the nurse would not attribute her hectic colour to anything other than the heat outside. 'We decided to have a proper lunch. What can I take over from you?'

'Well, Rita Cook has finished her laundry, we've fixed up her feet and she said to tell you she'll be in the Eating Place, having lunch,' Esther said to Titia as she stood in the doorway of the office. 'You're going to let her sleep here until she gets admitted to hospital?'

'That's right.'

Esther unbuttoned her loose white overall as she talked, revealing a cotton skirt and top underneath. Then she applied a little make-up to her tired, pale face, squinting at herself in the wall mirror. 'I've got to do a bit of grocery shopping,' she said, 'then I'm going to put my feet up in the park for fifteen minutes and eat my packed lunch. I may be a little late getting back.'

'Take your time, Esther,' Titia said. 'We're lucky today. I wasn't counting on having Dr Saxby here.'

'We're getting spoiled.' Esther laughed. 'Now, there are two guys waiting for you in the men's examination room. I thought you could do one and Dr Saxby could do the other.'

'Sure. Sounds like he's already started on one.' They could hear the reassuring murmur of Grant's voice.

'The one I've left for you is an illegal immigrant from Jamaica,' Esther went on, raking a brush through her hair. 'He admitted it—I didn't ask! He seemed eager to get it off his chest, wanted to know if there was a lawyer here who could help him get immigrant status. I said we did have a few lawyers available for that purpose, who donated their time. I said he could ask you about that.'

'Sure.'

'Anyway, he said he's an epileptic, doesn't feel well and doesn't have anywhere to stay,' Esther went on, as she rummaged in the desk drawer for her handbag. 'He had a small seizure this morning, so he said. He's got a cut lip and a few grazes on his face.' She swung her bag up onto her shoulder. 'He could have been in a fight. Anyway, Dr Lane, I've left that for you to decide. Seems like an OK guy to me. I think this heat, with the humidity, is enough for anyone to feel unwell, don't you? Not to mention having a chronic medical condition.'

'Yes, one's energy level certainly drops.'

'His name's Renfrew Brixton. He's as colourful as his name. He looks as though he could do with a good meal, too.'

'I'll sort him out.'

In her own office, Titia put on her lab coat again slowly and ran a brush through her hair. Then she took several calming breaths, blowing out the air slowly and fully, willing herself to relax.

'Phew!' she muttered to herself, thinking of Grant Saxby brushing his lips against her mouth. 'So that was what unfinished business meant.' It seemed incredible, in the utilitarian atmosphere of the examination room, that there had been such a flare-up of passion between them— if one could call it that. Perhaps it was just lust, a result on her part of not having much of a love life. Maybe she was about to crack. That thought was sobering.

Getting back into the swing of work was the sure way to put the interaction between herself and Grant to the back of her mind. Somehow she had to work with him for the remainder of the day. Then, maybe by next week she would be all right, would be able to confront him calmly.

With her stethoscope in her pocket and her medical bag in her hand, Titia went into the men's examination room and swished through the screening curtains of a cubicle, trying to ignore Grant's voice.

'Mr Brixton?' she said.

The man on the examination table was indeed colourful. On his head he wore a tall knitted hat into which his long hair was tucked. Tendrils of that hair straggled out all around the edge of the cap. He wore a ragtag assortment of clothes in rainbow colours, a pair of frayed jeans festooned with bright patches, a sleeveless denim jacket with embroidered place badges sown on it, and round his neck he had a selection of long, floaty scarves in bright patterns.

'That's me,' he said.

To Titia, he looked about twenty. He had the open-faced look of youth, yet he looked tired and somehow frightened, as though the effort at constant bravado, the type that so many young people displayed at the clinic, had worn him down so that he had few reserves left. Titia could tell the subtle—and not so subtle—signs of that street fatigue.

His sandalled feet were dusty, as though he had done

a lot of walking. He was tall and lean, with no fat on his body, it seemed. A cut on his lower lip oozed blood, while several grazes and swellings on other parts of his face gave the impression that he could have been in a fight. Or he could simply have fallen down and injured himself because of an epileptic seizure, as he had told Esther.

'I'm Dr Titia Lane,' she said, picking up the manila folder that Esther had left on the small mobile table-on-wheels that they used to move from bed to bed when they had to do an examination and take a history. The folder contained a single sheet of basic information, giving his name, his date of birth and 'No fixed address'. She saw that he was twenty-four years old.

'I see you have epilepsy, Mr Brixton, and you've run out of pills,' she said, reading the note the nurse had made on the diagnosis.

'Yeah,' he said, lifting his head up a little from where he was lying on the examination table. 'I haven't had any pills for about two months, didn't have money to buy any. But I've been OK up to this morning...haven't had any seizures. But today I felt real weird—like something was about to happen—so I went into the park and lay down under a bush.' He paused, his tongue gingerly exploring his cut lip.

'And you had a seizure?' Titia prompted gently.

'Yeah, I reckon I did, 'cause I don't remember much after that, except that I had a cut lip and all these bruises on my face. I used to have, like, two or three seizures a year before I started taking the pills. But then the pills didn't always agree with me so sometimes I got fed up with taking them...you know.'

'Yes, there are certain side-effects, not very pleasant,' Titia agreed, adding to the written notes. 'Were you taking one of the anti-epilepsy drugs? Or a sedative drug, a barbiturate?'

'It was an epilepsy drug.' He rummaged around in one of his pockets and came up with an empty plastic pill container with a printed label. 'Here.'

'Yes, I see,' Titia said, looking at it. 'So you got this here in Gresham.'

'Yeah, someone I know who works in a hospital got it for me for free,' he said. 'Now I don't have any money… No money, no pills.' He chuckled philosophically. 'So I came in here, didn't want to take any chances I can tell when something's coming on.'

'Well, Mr Brixton,' Titia said, 'I want to do a complete physical examination, as well as a history, then I want to take some blood for tests—you can get some liver problems sometimes from this type of medication. Then I want to see if we can get you to a hospital for an EEG – an electroencephalogram—which will show us your brain waves. That can tell us something about the nature of the condition that you have.'

'Yeah, I know,' he said. 'I had one once. That's how they knew what I had, see.'

'Well, it's time you had another one.'

Renfrew Brixton shifted uncomfortably on the narrow table. 'I haven't any health insurance. I'm an illegal.'

'I know,' Titia said. 'We have ways and means of getting things done when they have to be done. I understand you would like to speak to a lawyer.'

'Yeah…please,' he said.

It turned out that he did not have anywhere to stay for the night either. After Titia had done the physical examination and had taken some blood from a vein to put in the test tubes for the laboratory to do routine blood tests, she arranged for him to stay there for the night.

There was a six-bedded room they simply called the men's room, where he could stay until she had arranged the EEG for him at a hospital and worked out his medication. Sometimes the drugs that he had been taking suppressed the bone marrow and the subsequent production of blood cells, so when she got the results of the tests she would be able to prescribe a drug for him.

'Sometimes people with epilepsy do very well with just a sedative, phenobarbitol, although it does make you sleepy sometimes, and occasionally a bit depressed…if you tend to be somewhat depressed to begin with,' she added, looking at him assessingly, having observed that he was straining to appear considerably more upbeat than he felt.

'I ain't exactly cheerful right now,' he confessed.

'We'll get you sorted out,' she said kindly, 'both on the medical front and on the legal front. One of the legal guys who works with us is an immigration lawyer. He's a volunteer.'

'That's great,' he said, relaxing back with a sigh and crossing his legs in assumed nonchalance. 'I need all the help I can get.'

'We'll get you into hospital as soon as we can for that EEG,' she said. 'I expect you know about that already, Mr Brixton.'

'Yeah, sort of,' he said. 'Don't understand all the details.'

'Quite often the brain waves appear normal,' Titia explained. 'It may be only when you have a seizure that they appear abnormal. But we want to check anyway.'

'OK,' he said resignedly.

'Now, I'm going to have a go at your face,' she said, bending forward to get a better look at his oozing lip, angling a portable lamp so that it highlighted the damage.

'Are you telling me the truth about the seizure, Mr Brixton?' she said, 'or have you been in a fight? You see, I'm not going to give you medication if you don't need it…not until I get the result of the EEG, which could take some time.'

'I did have a seizure,' he said. 'Not that I don't get into fights, too, sometimes. I don't pick fights…I'm attacked, mostly. But not this time.'

'Fair enough,' Titia said. 'Now, I'm going to have to put two or three stitches in that lip.'

'Oh, heck,' he said, drawing back from her. 'I'm a bit of a coward.'

'It's all right,' she said, smiling at his candour. 'I'll inject a bit of local anaesthetic—you won't feel anything. Then I'll clean up those grazes. Have you got pain anywhere else?'

'No,' he said wearily, settling himself back and closing his eyes, 'nothing out of the ordinary.'

'I'll get a suture tray and make a start,' she said. 'Then we'll talk more about the medication. I'll probably give you some phenobarbitol, as I said.'

'Well, maybe I could use a bit of that right now,' he said.

As she left the room, Titia considered what she had just explained, that the drug also exacerbated any existing depression. They would have to take the risk. She would just give him a few pills until they had got some tests done.

She had no real evidence that he was clinically depressed, other than what he had told her and a gut feeling she had that he was lower in spirits than he was letting on. Having him stay at the Open Door for as long as necessary to get his health sorted out would do something to lessen the burden of his situation. He would get regular meals and they could keep him there until he had been able to talk to an immigration lawyer. At the Open Door clinic it was generally necessary to get things moving quickly. Many of the people who came in there were at, or near, crisis point.

'How's it going, Dr Lane?' Grant said to her in a low voice as she went past his office space to go to the main office to get a suture tray that was stored there. Maybe he had been listening to her conversation with Renfrew Brixton. 'You sound busy.'

'Oh, I am,' she said. 'In great demand all round.'

'Glad to see that you pull your weight around here.' He smiled in a way that smoothed out the tiredness in his face.

'Of course. I'm making sure you do as well,' she said, and left the room.

While she sutured Mr Brixton's lip very carefully with a very fine black silk thread on a fine curved needle, she could hear Grant talking softly to his next patient, taking a history. He was as good, as thorough, as competent as he had been all those years ago...

'I'm trying to make sure you don't have a scar, Mr Brixton,' she said. 'You wouldn't want to get a keloid scar here, just below your lip. Usually the lip itself heals up very well.'

'I know all about keloids,' he said. 'Got one or two on my body.'

Keloids were the thick, raised scars that people of African descent frequently developed after a cut to the skin. Sometimes those scars had to be surgically removed in the hope that the next scar that was left would be less noticeable.

'When I've done this, I'll show you where you can sleep,' she said.

*   *   *

It was time to go home before she knew it. It was four o'clock in the afternoon and it had been a long day. Two more nurses arrived to take over. She and Grant would go home, then later in the evening a volunteer doctor would come to cover the night shift. A lot of the time he, or she, got to sleep in the office. Most emergencies during the night went to an emergency department of a hospital, either to the University Hospital or to Gresham General, both teaching hospitals with very busy trauma units.

Both Rita Cook and Renfrew Brixton had been organized for hospital visits, one as an inpatient and the other as an outpatient. For now they would sleep at the church until their medical conditions had been sorted out. Also, Mr Brixton was to see a lawyer tomorrow.

Titia washed her hands and lower arms thoroughly with Betadine, an antiseptic iodine solution, at the sink in her makeshift office in preparation for going home. Her skin felt raw and dry from having been washed so many times throughout the day, every day, so when she had dried herself she creamed her skin generously with a soothing lotion.

'Dr Lane?' There was a knock on the screen and Grant came round the side.

'Hi,' she said.

'I'll say goodnight, Titia. See you next week here, if not before at the hospital. I'll get Rita Cook organized.' The verbal exchange they had had earlier after lunch might not have happened.

'Thank you. I appreciate that,' she said formally. His hair had been slicked back with water against the heat, making him look cool and sophisticated. He carried a black leather medical bag. Titia concentrated on smoothing lotion into her hands and arms, avoiding his astute gaze.

'Would you like to come for a drink?' he offered. 'Something long and cool.'

Titia put her used lab coat in a plastic bag and stuffed it into her medical bag, fighting the urge to agree. 'I think not right now,' she said crisply. 'Thanks, anyway.'

CHAPTER THREE

IT WAS not often that Laetitia did not sleep well these days. Yet that night sleep was elusive.

So often she counselled patients with insomnia to get up, rather than lie in bed, staring at the ceiling or into the darkness. Get up, make a warm drink—that was the formula.

Titia got out of bed and padded, with bare feet, into the kitchen of her small flat. The night was hot and humid. In the window of her sitting room the air-conditioner hummed on 'low', managing to get rid of the worst of the humidity that went with the heat. It was too hot, anyway, for a soporific hot drink.

In a saucepan Titia heated a tablespoonful of honey on the stove, then added a little brandy. When it was nicely blended she added the mixture to a glass of cold milk.

Out on the balcony of her fourth-floor apartment, which overlooked a wooded ravine area in an old, established area of central Gresham, the humidity and heat hit her like a blast from a Turkish bath. Thankfully, there was a slight breeze. It ruffled the thin cotton of her short nightdress. Sinking down into one of the plastic chairs that she kept out there, Titia knew that it would be a while before she could sleep. First, she had to think a few things through.

Sipping the drink, it reminded her sharply of the comforting hot drink—hot chocolate—that Grant Saxby had brought to her in that huge, cavernous church on that cool night when she had first met him. For a long time she had managed to put those details out of her mind.

In the vastness of that place their voices had echoed, as she had talked to him and he had listened, like the voices of lost souls. Certainly she had felt lost. She had been shivering from cold and shock, from having relived the trauma in the telling of the experience she had so recently been through with her family.

'You stay right here,' Grant had said, as they had been huddled together in the church pew. 'I'm going to get you a large mug of hot chocolate. Come to think of it, I could do with one, too.'

'Thanks,' she had said, aware of the emptiness and faintness of hunger. She had not eaten for hours, had been trying to conserve the small amount of money she had left. Although she had a bank card on her, she had not used it much for fear that she could be traced from it.

'Promise me you won't disappear while I go make it,' Grant said, seeming to unfold himself from the huddle they had been in, stretching his long legs in front of him.

'No...I won't go,' she promised. She couldn't put into words that she had a feeling of having come home somehow, a feeling that she could at last relax a bit, a feeling of warmth in the face of his caring.

'Hey, I don't know your name,' he said, after he had slipped out of the pew and was standing in the main aisle of the church. 'You'd better tell me your name.'

Warning bells rang in her head. It wasn't that she didn't trust him...she did, and she could not have analysed why very well... It was just that she had got into the habit of being anonymous for her own safety, she felt. She did not want Terry to find her.

'I would rather not tell you my name right now...if you don't mind,' she said. 'I...I just want to...um,'

'Keep a low profile?' he finished for her, as though that was what he was used to saying to maybe every second person he met at the Open Door refuge and clinic.

She nodded.

He smiled. 'If you won't tell me your name, I'll call you "runaway girl"...for now,' he said.

'All right,' she said, looking up at him. He had nice eyes, intelligent, perceptive, warm. 'Maybe I'll tell you some time.' She added the last bit shyly as she took another paper tissue to wipe the remains of the tears from her face.

'That's a bargain. Now, you stay right there.'

As he strode away from her down the aisle to the back of the church, where he disappeared towards the clinic rooms, she watched him. So there were a few good people left in the world, she thought, outside the familiar circle of her school friends and the two or three teachers she really liked at school.

All at once she could acknowledge that she was missing those people, that they must be wondering what on earth had happened to her. The first real glimmerings that what she had done was a kind of madness came to her then, as she leaned forward in her seat and put her arms on the back of the pew in front of her so that she could rest her head on them. What she had done had been on the spur of the moment; there had been no time to think things out. All she had known at the time had been that she had had to get away, that she had been in some sort of danger.

No doubt the police were looking for her. Her mother would have reported her missing initially, until the first letter she had written had been received. It was legal for a child to leave home at the age of sixteen, when the parents were no longer legally obliged to support him or her, but most did not leave home then unless something was wrong.

She shivered, in spite of the central heating in the church, glad that she was wearing thick wool tights and a roll-neck sweater with the short skirt and the heavy winter jacket she had had the foresight to grab before she had left home. Inadequate sleep and not enough food were taking their toll on her. All her other present worldly goods were in a knapsack. Often she thought of all the other clothes and conveniences she had at home, which she had hitherto taken entirely for granted.

It would be so good to sleep in a warm, clean, safe place. Last night she had slept in a secluded doorway near a park with another young woman who had befriended her and who had talked in her sleep.

The young doctor's returning footsteps interrupted her weary reverie.

'Hey,' he said, 'we're in luck. I've got two huge chocolate-chip muffins for us, too. They're fresh, just baked this afternoon. I'm pretty starved myself.'

'Thank you,' she said appreciatively. 'I hope I'm not taking you away from your work.'

'No, I've finished for the night. I was just about to go home when you came.' He handed her a mug. 'Careful, it's hot. I try to work on the evenings when I have a day off the next day...otherwise I couldn't hack it,' he said candidly. 'I've got a few things I want to do tomorrow—something at the hospital, plus a lecture at the university, although I could skip both if I wanted to.'

There was something sweetly boyish about him. Yet he was far from boyish in the work he was doing, in the shrewd way he had summed her up. This was all new to her, but to him it was something he saw almost every day, she realized.

Titia shot surreptitious glances at him as they devoured the muffins and sipped the hot drinks like two children who had sneaked down to the kitchen for a forbidden midnight feast. He seemed to have entered into her world so that there was no difference between them at all.

'This is the most wonderful hot chocolate I've ever had,' she said truthfully.

'There's something about drinking in a church like this that makes it special—a bit like camping out.' He was trying to put her at ease, to help her take her mind off her ordeal, her loss and her dilemma. As Titia cupped her hands around the hot mug, she acknowledged that he was succeeding.

'Well, runaway girl,' he said, 'I guess you haven't got anywhere to stay for the night. It's getting pretty late. You would like to stay here, I guess?'

'Could I? You're right, I…don't have anywhere to stay. Last night I slept in a doorway.'

As he sat next to her she could see his ID badge, with his photograph on it, which was clipped to the breast pocket of his lab coat. Her eyes strayed to it, squinting in the dim light. Following her line of vision, he unclipped the badge and handed it to her silently. Unabashed, she read it carefully. Maybe she wasn't very experienced in life, but she was streetwise. No matter how much you liked someone, or felt that you could trust them just after you had met them, you still had to be very, very careful, had to check them out—to make sure they were who they said they were, for a start. You should never break the rules for your own safety…

'Grant Crawford Saxby,' she read. 'Medical Student (4th year), Faculty of Medicine, Gresham University, Gresham, Ontario.' Underneath that information was the date the card had been issued. The coloured photograph was better then the usual mug shot—at least she could recognize him easily. At the bottom of the laminated card a sticker had been affixed, bearing the information, 'Volunteer, Open Door Clinic, St Barnabas's Church, Gresham.'

Satisfied, she handed back the card. 'Crawford?' she said.

When he grinned, she smiled back. 'That's my mother's maiden name,' he explained. 'Not many people know about it. That's the way I like it. I don't want them calling me Craw.'

There was a sweet moment of awareness between them, before he abruptly clipped the ID badge back on his lab coat.

'You can stay here,' he said. 'I'll fix something up for you. Tell me, does your mother know where you are?' He finished the last mouthful of muffin and crumpled the paper, then drained the last of his hot chocolate.

'She doesn't know exactly where I am,' Titia admitted, feeling again the enormity of what she had done as she was subjected to his steady scrutiny. 'I send her a note once a week to let her know that I'm OK.'

Unable to sustain eye contact with him, even in the dim interior of the church, she looked away, tears gathering again in her eyes. Not only was she missing her friends, she was missing her mother. Those feelings had earlier been obscured by resentment and anger that her mother would take up with a man like Terry. Then there was the terrible grief...

'Does your mother know that the guy—what's his name? Terry? That he hit you, threatened you?' Grant said, with gentle persistence.

'Yeah,' she said. She was beginning to feel a little defensive at his persistence as he made her feel that what she had done had been reactionary rather than thought out. Maybe she should have gone to the police, maybe she should not have left her mother with that guy. There were too many maybes. 'I told her in the first letter I sent…and I told her I was staying with a friend. I didn't tell her which friend.'

'She must have been worried sick about you. She must still be.' His tired eyes focussed on her face, as though trying to figure her out, she thought. Maybe he was judging her, judging her for doing such a dumb thing. A little resentfully, she stared back.

'I did think about that,' she said, something of her former spirit surfacing. 'I didn't mean to hurt her. She sure hurt me…' When her voice broke he put his arm round her and pulled her head down to rest on his shoulder.

'It's OK,' he said. 'It's OK.'

For a long time they did not speak as she struggled to control herself. 'I have a sister who's a first-year resident in obstetrics at University Hospital,' he said at last. 'Her name's Loretta. She has a room in the medical staff and nurses' residence at the hospital, and I know she's on call tonight so she won't be in the room. I'll call her and tell her that you will be in her room…she won't mind.'

'Are you sure?'

'Yes. That's better than you staying here. You would have to share with half a dozen other people, I expect, sleeping on the floor. Loretta's going on vacation to Italy for two weeks, leaving in a couple of days. I'm pretty sure she won't mind if you use her room. She lives permanently with our parents so this is just a convenience for her,' he said.

'That's…that's nice of you,' Titia said, feeling tremendous relief but at the same time wondering whether she ought to accept, whether there would be any strings attached. Young as she was, she was not stupid.

'I'll have to trust you, and you'll have to trust me,' he said, no doubt reading her thoughts with accuracy. 'And so will Loretta. I don't live there myself.'

'Thank you,' she said, meaning it with all her heart.

'Maybe in the two weeks Loretta's away,' he said, 'you can get yourself sorted out.'

She nodded.

'Are you on drugs?' he asked abruptly.

'No!' She pulled away from him to eye him fiercely, righteous indignation welling up in her. 'Of course not!' Couldn't he tell just by looking at her that she was just a schoolgirl who had led a rather sheltered life? But, then, she wasn't a schoolgirl right now—was she? She had missed several weeks of school, was in an academic limbo at a time when her education was important. Somehow she swallowed her indignation, breathing deeply.

'Sorry.' He shrugged in apology as she glared at him. 'I had to ask. It's a standard question here. Do you drink?'

'Is that another standard question?'

'Mmm.'

'Well, the answer's no,' she said tightly, 'unless by "drink" you mean the very occasional consumption of a glass of wine with a meal.' The mention of wine conjured up thoughts of meals with her parents in restaurants, to celebrate birthdays, or something, and her voice wavered.

'Sorry,' he repeated, as he gently put his arm around her shoulders again and eased her head down so that she was resting against him. Stiffly, she resisted the gesture at first, then she gradually gave in to her need.

'There are one or two other standard questions,' he said, after a few minutes, 'but I won't embarrass you by

asking them.' There was a smile in his voice. Titia
guessed that one question would be about AIDS. She said
nothing.

'We'd better go, it's getting late,' he said. 'I've got an
old car that's just about roadworthy. We'll go in that.'

But it was a while before they moved, relaxing in the
glow engendered by the hot drinks and the comforting
warmth and quiet of the old building. Instinctively, Titia
knew that he was in some way deriving comfort from
her presence, too, as though they had recognized a need
in each other, and had seen that they could complement
each other in some way...a strange belonging. She could
not put it into words—it was just something that she felt.
Gradually some of the hurt in her began to lessen. Up to
then she had resisted thinking much about her father, how
she mourned him. It had been unbearable so she had focussed instead on her dilemma of being a runaway. Now
she let tentative thoughts of him creep into her mind...

'You can call me Tricia,' she said softly, after long
moments when they had sat in companionable silence.

'Is that right?' he teased her. 'And I was just getting
used to "runaway girl". I guess it's too much to ask what
Tricia is short for?'

She laughed then...she actually laughed!

'It is,' she said.

That was the beginning of their peculiarly intense yet
innocent relationship. There was a passion in knowing
each other. Yet he never touched her except in comfort,
never kissed her except quickly on the cheek or on the
forehead, as a brother might have done on saying goodbye. In the end she stayed for three weeks in that small
room. During that time her feelings for Grant Saxby were
such that she knew she would never forget him...

Loretta, his sister, came over to the room for a few minutes when they first arrived in the multi-storey modern building that had been built for medical staff and nurses in a quiet side street across from University Hospital. Not many nurses actually lived there, preferring to have apartments away from the hospital, so rooms were let to other professionals and post-graduate university students. Titia learned this on the journey over.

The buildings were, Grant Saxby told her, connected by underground tunnels, which were very convenient in winter when there was snow on the ground or there was a blizzard and the temperature was ten degrees below freezing.

'Use anything you want,' Loretta said to her, sizing her up astutely, apparently deciding she was harmless. 'Shampoo, soap…you'll find everything you want somewhere here. There's a bathroom across the hall. There are clean sheets on the bed, by the way.' Then she rummaged in a drawer and brought out a long, oversized T-shirt. 'You can use this as a nightshirt.'

'Thank you.' Titia took it shyly, aware that Grant had a slight smile on his face while appearing not to actually look at what was going on as he stood a little awkwardly in the room.

Grant's sister looked very much like him, the same dark hair, the intelligent blue-grey eyes, the fair skin. Titia watched her while she took a bathrobe out of the built-in closet. 'Here's a robe you can use,' she said, handing it to Titia. Then she gathered up soap, talcum powder, shampoo and baby lotion, and added them to the pile Titia had accumulated in her arms.

'There's only one thing I ask,' she added, just as her beeper went off, summoning her back to work. 'Please, don't lose the key.'

'I won't. Thank you…I'm grateful,' Titia hesitantly offered her thanks, feeling it was inadequate.

'Must go,' Loretta had said. 'Baby brother will take care of you.'

Before her tired brother could make a rejoinder, she was out of the small, comfortable room she had given over to Titia.

'She patronizes me, and spoils me, too,' Grant said, settling himself into an armchair.

'She seems very nice,' Titia said. 'You're lucky to have a sister. I'm an only child…if I can still call myself that. Right now, I sure don't feel like a child, or a teenager. I feel about ninety years old.'

'The same goes for me right now,' he said, stretching out his long legs and putting his head wearily back against the chair, closing his eyes.

'Thank you for all this,' she said.

'It's the least I can do,' he said. 'I feel for you. Sympathy and empathy are not much good without action…so I've discovered in this doctoring business, although just listening is action, too.'

'Yes.'

'Well, runaway girl, have a bath. I'll wait here until I've seen you settled, then I'll give you my address and phone number so you can contact me. I'll come by tomorrow, show you where you can have breakfast in the hospital cafeteria. I shall expect you to keep in touch. Promise me that you won't take off until you've sorted yourself out.'

'Yes, I do promise,' she said, hugging the accoutrements for her bath against her chest, realizing again how kind he was…how attractive, too.

'Take your time with the bath,' he said. 'Don't rush because of me. I'll just sleep. I've trained myself to sleep any time, any place, when necessary. That's a good trait to have in my job.'

Titia took him at his word. While the bath water was running, she used the baby lotion to cream off the eye makeup which had run in black streaks down her cheeks.

When she looked in the mirror her appearance shocked her—the pasty skin, the large, haunted eyes, the hair that stuck up in tufts, stiff with the dirt of dusty streets. It had a blue sheen on it that looked very fake, from the stuff that she sprayed on it…the latest fad. Now it looked ridiculous to her, as did the matte black dye she had on her hair underneath the blue. It all looked fake, too dark for the tone of her skin. Well, she would wash the blue out, soften her hair back to its normal consistency.

Angry at herself for getting into the situation she was in, she plastered her face with the lotion, then scrubbed at it with tissues. Being back in a clean, warm, civilized place was somehow shocking her back into reality. Sooner or later she was going to have to face up to the reality that her father was gone, that her mother was living with a predatory man who might harm her.

Alarm for her mother took the place of the fear for herself which had up till then been at the forefront of her concern. She was warm and safe, and would soon be clean again. It was possible to think of other things. There was a terrible fear that maybe she had left some things too late. Concern for her mother seemed to settle right in her chest, in the region of her heart, like an actual pain.

The hot bath was wonderful so she took her time about it, shampooing her hair vigorously as she sat in the water, feeling the oil and dirt wash out of it. Later, as she dried her hair with the conveniently placed wall-mounted hairdryer, she looked at the transformation of herself. The girl who stared back at her from the mirror—the black smudges gone, the tufts of hair transformed to a shining mass of blow-dried sophistication—was something more than the schoolgirl she had been such a short while ago. In that time, something had happened to her, an innocence had gone. Her plump, rounded face had hollowed out. She was a woman now; she knew that instinctively.

Grant was asleep when she went back quietly to the room, his head lolling to one side, his hair untidily across his forehead. For a few minutes she looked at him, shyly. Often she had dreamed about having a boyfriend like him, good-looking, intelligent, sensitive as well... He seemed all that she had ever wanted. But she was too young for him, too inexperienced. And no doubt he thought that what she had done had been impulsive, perhaps stupid...even though he had so clearly understood. A young man like Grant Saxby, with a great future in front of him, would not want a girl who had gone to live on the street, she thought, as her eyes explored him.

She was coming round to the idea that maybe she should have found some other way to deal with it all, a way that would not have left her mother with a load of anxiety.

Just then he woke up, to find her standing in front of him, staring. Their eyes met and locked, then his eyes went over her with such a look of surprise that she blushed a fiery red.

'Hey,' he said softly, straightening up slowly in the chair, 'you look different...beautiful. So, runaway girl, this is the real you. Hmm?'

'Well...' She smiled, wishing her cheeks didn't burn so, liking his words. 'This isn't the real colour of my hair.'

'I figured that,' he said, laughing. He got up and stretched. 'I've written my address and number here.' He indicated a piece of paper that he had put on the bedside table. 'And Loretta's pager number, if you should need to get in touch with her. I don't think anyone will call her here as she's got the pager.'

Titia nodded. 'Thanks.'

'You get a good night's sleep,' he said. 'I'll phone you in the morning, then I'll come and take you for breakfast. OK?'

She nodded again, trying to will the colour in her cheeks to subside. The robe was belted tightly around her body, yet she was aware of her bare feet, her physical vulnerability, in the face of his obvious masculinity as he looked at her with veiled admiration and interest in his eyes, an interest that was not that of a doctor with a patient. After all, she was not exactly his patient. The relationship between them was ambiguous, to say the least, she thought as she looked back at him.

'Will you be all right?' he added softly.

'I expect so.'

'I'm less than half a mile away from here,' he said, 'if you need anything, or if you feel you can't hack it by yourself. So don't hesitate to call me. I'm used to being called any time of the day or night.' He added that bit ruefully. 'So it's no sweat.'

'All right,' she said. 'Thanks again.'

He picked up his medical bag from where he had left it on the floor.

'Goodnight, then runaway girl. Sleep tight.' With that, he leaned forward and gave her a quick kiss on the cheek. Then he opened the door decisively and in a moment he was gone.

With the warmth of his kiss on her cheek, Titia put down the stuff she was holding and got into the bed, robe and all, snuggling down under the covers. She left the light on, not wanting to be in the dark. In the glow of the bedside lamp the piece of paper on which he had written his telephone number seemed to be the connecting link between them. If she needed him, she could just reach out to the telephone beside the lamp and punch out those seven numbers.

As she crossed her arms around herself in a hug of acute loneliness, tempered by the memory of him, that piece of paper was a lifeline.

When you were living on the street you tended to wake up at the crack of dawn. There was noise from the increasing traffic, delivery vans, people starting to go to work, the world waking up. Also, you got up so that you could go somewhere to get a free breakfast at one of the hostels. Apart from those things, you haven't slept very well anyway.

From recently acquired habit, Titia's eyelids snapped open early, to find a stream of grey light seeping through a crack in the curtains of Loretta's room. For a few seconds she was totally disorientated, then the realization came to her swiftly that the reason she was warm and lying in a clean, cosy bed was that she had been 'rescued' by a young medical student. A flood of relief came over her as the realization hit her. She was all right, and she was going to stay all right. There was also a sense that she had slept very well. The bedside light was still burning.

The night before, she had noticed a laundry room at the end of the corridor so now she got up quickly and, taking the key to the room, some coins from her knapsack and her bundled clothes, she padded down there silently. There was no one else up, although she suspected that if there were any doctors or nurses on her floor they would be getting up early. Maybe they would query her presence.

She put everything washable she had into the washing machine, using coins to operate it and to buy detergent from a slot machine. It was very satisfying to see her dirty clothes whirling round and round in soapy water. While her stuff was drying she would write a letter to her mother, saying that she would be in touch soon, that she was safe and staying with a friend. Later, after breakfast, she would find a place to post it.

When Grant phoned she was ready for him, dressed in her clean clothes, the bed neatly made.

'Hi,' he said. 'Good morning.'

'Hi,' she said.

'Did I wake you?'

'No. I've been up for a long time.'

'I'll be there in about fifteen minutes to take you to breakfast in the hospital cafeteria. You must be pretty hungry.'

'I am,' she said shyly. 'Will it be all right for me to eat there? I mean, I'm not staff, am I?' Actually, she was shy about going into a hospital cafeteria, where there would be people who knew Grant. Surely they would wonder where she came in, why she was there so early in the day, not exactly the time for visitors to the hospital.

'Sure, it will be fine,' he said reassuringly. 'For one thing, the cafeteria's open to non-staff so no one will notice you. It's a huge place, you'll be lost in the crowd. Quite a lot of business people who work in the offices around there have breakfast in the cafeteria.'

'Oh, that's all right, then,' she said, relieved somewhat. 'Um, I'm afraid I haven't got much money on me.'

'I'm going to treat you—don't worry about that. Afterwards we're going to talk about your problem, how to solve it. Is that a bargain?' he said, decisively.

'OK,' she said. If he could sort out her problems, good luck to him. She was at a stalemate, she had to admit that. She didn't know how to backtrack, or how to go forward.

'Wait in the room,' Grant said. 'I'll come up to get you.'

It would be easy enough to contact her mother, she knew that, but she did not want to go home if Terry was still there. And she had no way of knowing whether he was there. Ever since she had left home she had telephoned her house at least twice a week to satisfy herself that her mother was all right, then she had hung up without speaking, calling from a different public call box each time so that she could not be traced. Only once had Terry answered, at the very beginning. Gradually, she had come to hope that he was no longer there.

Only once had she gone to her own street, after dark, and waited around near one end of it, under some trees, watching her house. The lights had been on. No one had gone in or come out. She had stood in the cool evening, tears running down her cheeks wanting to go in, remembering the days when she had been younger, waiting for her father to come home from work.

Fear of Terry had held her back. Surely her mother would see that he was just a predatory opportunist.

Obsessively, she had mulled over the events of the recent weeks many times. When Grant Saxby knocked on the door, she was doing it again.

'Wow,' he said when she opened the door to him, 'you sure look different again.' There was an admiring light in his eyes as he looked her over, a gesture that brought a lightness to her heart.

'It's called clean,' she said, laughing, surprising herself again. 'I took advantage of the laundry here.'

'I'm glad you did,' he said, standing casually in the doorway. This morning he was more formally dressed in grey pants and a light shirt with a tie under a warm jacket against the October chill. 'You look great. I might not have recognized you in different clothes. Sleep obviously agrees with you, too.'

Titia was aware then of her soft, clean hair brushing silkily against her cheeks and neck, her scrubbed skin, the good feeling of being clean all over, knowing that she was not unattractive. 'You don't look too bad yourself,' she said, something of her former youthful cheekiness coming to the surface. A few days ago she had thought that her sense of humour had gone for ever.

'Thanks,' he said, grinning. He picked up a thick strand of her hair, ran it through his fingers. 'You're pretty. Has anyone ever told you that? If not, they should have.'

'A few,' she said. Hopefully, he wasn't going to be patronizing. Nonetheless, she liked his words.

Seeing her expression, he smiled again. 'Don't worry, I'm not the smarmy type.'

'Thank God for that,' she said boldly.

'You *are* pretty. Don't be embarrassed. You need to know how to take a compliment because in the future you're going to get lots of them.'

'I'm not embarrassed,' she said hotly. 'Are we going, or what? I've got the key in my pocket.'

They took the elevator down to the sub-basement of the building, then walked through a tunnel where thick water pipes and heating pipes and ducts encroached upon the ceiling space, making it rather claustrophobic.

'A bit spooky,' Titia said, walking close to Grant.

'Yeah. It's pretty safe, though, you won't get mugged down here. It's a great way to get over to the hospital in the dead of winter. At least the morgue and autopsy room isn't off this tunnel.'

'I wish you hadn't said that,' she admonished him.

'Sorry.' He squeezed her arm. 'The cafeteria's on the main floor, not far from the main hospital lobby. Was the room OK? Did you sleep well?'

'Yes, to both questions. It's really great. Can I really stay there for two weeks?'

'Sure,' he said, striding beside her, swinging his black leather medical bag. 'And we won't kick you out at the end of that time if things haven't been sorted out for you.'

'Have you done this before? Taken in people like me?'

'A few times,' he admitted, 'but I and my sister don't make a habit of it. We choose carefully who we can help—you get an instinct for those who want to be helped. There's no point in flogging a dead horse. I get the impression that you're a bright girl, that you're missing school. Am I right, Tricia?'

She had to admit it. 'Yes.'

'Look, after breakfast I have to go to some rounds here at the hospital—'

'Rounds?'

'A group of medical students meets with a few staff doctors and some interns and residents-in-training to go to see a few patients, interesting cases, then we discuss them afterwards…,or maybe we just meet to discuss patients that we've already seen,' he explained.

'I'm not sure that I like hospitals,' she said quietly. 'They can be very sad places.' The memories of her father, which she had tried to block out, came edging their way back, painfully, into her consciousness. A lot of the time she managed to think of him as he had been when she was growing up—teaching her to ride a two-wheeler bicycle, playing with the family dog, the times he had helped her to sort out school and personal problems... Those problems all seemed so innocent and petty now.

Grant Saxby cast a quick glance at her. 'I know,' he said. 'They are also places of great hope. They save lives, they improve the quality of life for so many people. Can you imagine what life was like without modern hospitals in the bad old days?'

'No, I can't really. I guess we take things for granted.'

They took another elevator, on the other side of the tunnel, up to the main floor of the hospital. Titia was amazed to see how busy the place was early in the morning. Doctors and nurses were hurrying about, walking along the wide corridors, looking important or harassed, their white coats flapping as they sped by. Porters pushed large carts of clean linen or supplies in cardboard boxes.

The cafeteria, as huge as Grant had said, was busy with staff having late breakfasts, serving themselves, then carrying their trays to the tables. She and Grant blended into the crowd; no one took the slightest notice of her. Overwhelmed at first by the variety and amount of food that was available, she chose some grilled bacon, scrambled eggs and hot croissants, a cup of tea and a glass of orange juice.

Grant found a small table for two near the side of the room. Feeling rather overwhelmed by the bustle of the place, the loud hum of conversation, Titia bent her head over her plate and began to eat.

'I could meet you for lunch,' Grant said, 'in the main hospital lobby, which is very close to this cafeteria, if you would like me to. Say twelve-thirty?'

She nodded.

'After rounds I've got a couple of lectures at the university. Then this afternoon I've got some voluntary labs. I may go to those for a short while. Will you be OK on your own? You can go back to the room, of course. I don't think Loretta will need to come back there for anything.'

'I'll be all right.' She nodded. 'Thank you for all you've done for me, I do appreciate it. I...I might go back there and sleep. That's something I haven't had enough of for a while.'

'Great!' He smiled across at her. 'Half past twelve it is, then.'

That was the beginning of their real closeness, the affinity she would feel with him. They established a routine—while he had to work and attend lectures, she slept, did her laundry, went to museums and art galleries, then met him for meals. For part of each evening he would stay with her, sometimes reading or studying in the room.

A lot of the time she had vivid dreams about things that had happened to her over the past few weeks, including the people she had met in the hostels and on the street. For the first few days after she'd left home she had stayed with friends, then had left because she knew that their mothers would know something was up and would inform her mother. Now she kept in touch with those friends by writing letters to them, not giving an address, making arrangements to telephone them at certain times.

In between times, she and Grant talked and talked. Most of the time she did the talking and he listened, having drawn her out with skilful questioning, while they lounged in Loretta's room. Sometimes she sat on the floor with him, sometimes she curled up in the armchair.

'You must speak to your mother, Tricia,' Grant said to her one day. 'This way of going on is crazy. She must be going mad with anxiety. For all you know, that guy Terry may have moved on. Do you want me to find out?'

'No! No, I don't,' she said emphatically. From that moment she was beginning to realize that she felt a sense of shame at what she had done. 'Maybe I should have dealt with it in some other way, I know that... Maybe gone to a school counsellor, asked advice from one of my friends' parents...I don't know.' While she sat on the floor, her back propped up against the bed, Grant sat in the chair, his legs comfortably crossed, looking like a benign inquisitor.

'Hmm,' he said, noncommittally.

Titia darted small sideways glances at him, not really able to tell what he thought of her, whether he was judging her. 'Maybe,' she went on, 'I should have gone to the church minister—where we go to assemblies from school—or my own doctor. She's a very understanding woman.'

'Why didn't you, then?' Grant murmured.

'I don't know,' Titia replied a trifle irritably, sensitive to any implied criticism. 'Because I didn't, that's all!'

'It's OK, sweetheart,' Grant murmured. 'I don't mean to be critical. I just want to understand.'

'I thought you did understand,' she shot back. There was a vague understanding that she had acted as she had done because her father was no longer there, that she couldn't take any more.

'Running away,' she said hesitantly, thinking it out, 'seemed like the natural thing to do at the time. I...needed to be on my own, to make my own decisions...but not necessarily to be alone. I can't say I wanted that.'

'I do understand most of it,' he said, leaning forward.

'Why are you helping me, anyway?' she demanded. 'I

appreciate it very, very much…but I didn't ask you, did I? I mean, if you're getting fed up with me, I can go.'

'I'm not getting fed up.' He articulated each word carefully. 'And I don't have any hidden agendas. I'm helping you because I want to…and because it's my job. I don't like doing things by half-measures—you know, like discharging a sick person onto the street when you know they've got nowhere to go. Maybe I have a pathological need to help people, I don't know. What I do know is that having taken on a job, I want to do it one hundred per cent, to see it through. You know…not just do the easy bit, then back off.'

Titia sighed and nodded. More than anything at that moment she wanted to be there with him. For the first time since her father had had the accident she felt reasonably secure and cared for.

'I just want to persuade you that it's time to call a halt to this,' he said. 'You see, Tricia, adults—mothers—have needs, too. They're human like we are. Sometimes they just put up a brave front so that they won't let us down. Your mother must be going through hell, only hearing from you once a week, not knowing exactly where you are.'

Titia shrugged, looking at the floor as he went on in the same vein.

'We can't just see them as the embodiment of roles in relation to ourselves. They are people in their own right. They have needs, wants, ambitions, fears—everything that we have. They're vulnerable, just like we are in some ways,' he said earnestly.

'Yes, I know,' she said with a sigh, fighting guilt and tears. 'I…understand what you're saying, but I can't *feel* it—you know? All I can think of at the moment, really, is myself.'

'Yes, I do know,' he said quietly. 'That's because all you can feel at the moment is your own pain. It would be better if you could share it with someone.'

'Isn't that what I'm doing with you?' she said defiantly, to hide the prick of tears in her eyes. What he said was true—she knew that instinctively. Doing it was another matter.

'It's a beginning,' he said.

'My mother thinks I'm with friends,' she said.

'How do you know that when you haven't spoken to her?' he persisted quietly.

'Well, I don't know for sure,' she admitted, 'but I do phone friends who sometimes speak to my mother and tell her I'm all right. I believe what they tell me.'

'Do you think that's enough for her?'

'As I said, right now all I can really think about is myself—that's all I can handle. This is the way I decided to do it. Maybe it's wrong...' she said, her exasperation rising. 'You're beginning to sound like a psychology book.'

He laughed. 'Sorry,' he said, 'I'll shut up for a bit.' He got up from the chair and stretched his tall, lean body, like a cat—a very aristocratic cat, she thought, maybe a Siamese. Her family had had a Siamese cat once, loved, spoiled and petted...

'Good,' she said, remaining on the floor.

'I'm going to make some coffee or tea,' he said. 'Want some?'

'I'd rather have hot chocolate,' she said, knowing that she was sounding a bit like a demanding child but unable to stop herself. Maybe he was trying to fill the role of her father, the insight came to her. Well, he had a long way to go.

'Your wish is my command.' He put his hands together and bowed low in front of her so she had to smile.

'Promise me something,' he said. 'Promise that if you leave here, without telling me that you're going, you'll write to me afterwards, or call me, at least once to let me know that you're all right.'

He sat down on the edge of the bed, looking at her, his forehead creased in a frown, while she swivelled round so that her back was supported by the dressing table and she could look at him. With seeming casualness, she reclined there in what she thought was a suitably defiant stance. All of a sudden he was getting altogether too bossy, she thought.

'Why?' she said, a little sullenly, giving him a wide-eyed stare, not smiling, trying to stare him out. It was not easy. If only he weren't so good-looking, if only he didn't make her feel fluttery inside when he looked at her like that, all concerned and earnest.

'Because I'd worry like hell about you,' he said. 'That's how I know what your mother must be feeling.'

Titia lowered her eyes. It was difficult to be defiant with him, she considered, because he was for real. Even when what he said implied criticism of her. Yes...he wasn't the fake sort. There had been a number of fake people in her life, people who had let her down.

'Sure. I promise,' she said.

One day, not too far away, she was to remember that promise, because she decided to leave. But it was not because he had become too bossy, or anything like that. It was because she realized that she was maybe getting too involved with him, had come to rely on him too much.

It was no good, of course. There could never be anything in it. She was quite a bit younger then he was, a mere schoolgirl still; maybe he would laugh at her if he knew. Maybe he really thought she was naïve and silly to have done what she did, although she had no proof of that... Maybe he would think it if he knew what she felt about him. Anyway, a young man with his ambitions, his career before him, would not want to align himself personally with a runaway girl.

Yes, she had to move on...

Dr Laetitia Lane drained the last few dregs of her milky drink. Already the brandy in the drink was having the required soporific effect on her. Perhaps now she would sleep, so she got up, moving languidly in the heat of high summer. The sitting room was pleasantly cool as she went back into it, closing the door to the balcony behind her.

Maybe Dr Grant Saxby, ensconced in his house in an old, charming, well-established neighbourhood—he had told her that much—was having difficulty sleeping, too.

One other thing he had done for her when she had been sixteen had been to alleviate her fear of hospitals. They had toured the whole place together, many times. He had talked to her about patients, had taken her around the operating rooms on a weekend evening when not many staff were about, had taken her over the emergency department.

'I wouldn't mind being a doctor,' she had murmured one day.

'You'll have to go back to school, then,' he had said.

Well, she had gone back to her school, back to her mother, who had told her that Terry had left, had been kicked out, the day after he had hit her. One day she had just picked up the telephone in Loretta's civilized room, which had made everything seem normal again, and had dialled her home. 'Mummy?' she had said, when the voice had answered at the other end. In moments they had both been crying. It had been all over, that part of it at least.

All that angst had really been for nothing. But she didn't regret it now, not really. During that time she had grown up. She had met Grant Saxby.

From then on she had worked single-mindedly to get into medical school. On an emotional level she had both cherished the memory of Grant Saxby, had sort of pet-rified him in her mind, and at the same time had tried to forget him.

Laetitia stood, staring out of the window at the night sky, where a few stars were just visible. One other thing seemed left over from those days...she did still have some emotional attachment to him.

Rita Clark

CHAPTER FOUR

RITA COOK was admitted to University Hospital two days later, on the Wednesday in the second week of a sweltering August, her admission having been arranged by Grant. More than ever, Titia was glad that he was connected once again to the Open Door Clinic. That clinic needed all the influence it could get.

On the Thursday, when she was working at the hospital, having put in her three days at the clinic, Titia went up during her lunch-break to see Rita, who was on one of the general medical floors.

'Oh, Dr Lane!' Rita exclaimed with delight when Titia entered the four-bedded ward. 'It's so great to see you! Here I am, in all my glory.' She gave a wheezy laugh, sitting up in bed and wearing a pale blue hospital gown, obviously absolutely delighted, unlike some people, to be in the hospital. Maybe it was because she did not have a disease that was immediately life-threatening and because, as a homeless person, she was going to enjoy every moment of the free food, good bed and air-conditioned comfort of the room she was sharing with other people.

'How are you, Rita?' Titia walked to the bedside and took her patient's thin hand in her own. 'This is my lunch-break so I thought I'd just pop up for a quick visit.'

Rita's wispy, thinning hair was clean and carefully combed. 'I'm glad you did,' she said, grinning. 'It's great to see a familiar face. I feel much better since I've been in here, even though it's early days. This fluid they're giving me…' she paused to indicate the intravenous line that was transfusing fluid into a vein from a hanging plastic IV bag '…must be doing something very positive for me, as well as a few regular meals I've had.'

'That's very good to hear. I suppose I can't really call you my patient any more, can I?' Titia said. 'Not while you're in here, anyway, as I work in the emergency department. So I guess I have to be in the capacity of visitor.'

'You sure look the part of doctor,' Rita said, looking at Titia's light green scrub suit which she wore under a white lab coat.

'Well, give me the low-down, Rita,' Titia said. 'Make it snappy because I've got to get back to the overdoses and the road traffic accidents.'

'Eek! Spare me the details, Dr Lane.' Rita shuddered with mock horror. 'Well, that nice Dr Saxby is looking after me,' she said, her tired face lighting up. 'He's doing things with the insulin dose.'

'That's great! I hoped he would be looking after you himself,' Titia said, 'then he can continue to see you at the clinic. Of course, I hope we'll have you in an apartment by then.'

'Maybe you will at that,' Rita said, an admiring note in her voice. 'I'm beginning to hold out a bit of hope, anyway. He doesn't mess about, believe me. I've already had lots of blood taken for tests, although I don't know what they're all for.'

'Good,' Titia said. 'That's what I wanted—a thorough work-up. When you have diabetes your whole body chemistry can get out of whack.'

'I said to the nurse on the IV team this morning, when she came to take some more blood, "You're a real blood-sucker." That's what I said.' Rita chuckled again, her eyes gleaming, obviously enjoying the attention she was getting. 'And I said to her, ''Don't take too much, I haven't got much to begin with!'' She did laugh at that. I expect they've heard it all before, don't you? The same old jokes, eh? Anyway, that's me all over. I do like a joke. It makes the world go round, eh?'

'Yes, it does. We have to keep a sense of humour,' Titia agreed.

'We do, that,' Rita said. 'I've had a shower this morning and washed my hair, then, as soon as I'd done that, someone came with a wheelchair to take me for an X-ray, just of my chest. The lady down there said they wanted to do a mammogram too...she explained all about it. They are going to fit me in as soon as they can.'

'That's good. You might as well get as much done as possible while you're in here.'

'I'm going to see a gynaecologist and a nutritionist, and a...whatsit? Endo...something?' Rita said, frowning in concentration.

'Endocrinologist?' Titia suggested.

'That's it!' Rita confirmed. 'Dr Saxby said he would sort out my hormone levels, my thyroid and other things, to see whether the balance is normal...or something. He explained it all to me, although a few things went in one ear and out the other. He's such a nice guy. Oh! Talk of the devil!'

When Titia turned, Grant was coming into the room, and his eyes were on her before he diverted his attention to his patient. Like her, he was attired in the ubiquitous scrub suit, the most comfortable attire in the humid, hot summer weather, even though he, being in Internal Medicine, did not have to do any scrubbing.

'Hello, Rita.' He came up to the bed. 'Hi, there, Dr

Lane. It's good to see you both. Maybe I can kill two birds with one stone.'

'Eh?' Rita said, smiling up at him. 'What does that mean?'

'It means I can tell Dr Lane all that's been happening to you,' he said.

'She hasn't much time,' Rita said pertly, blossoming under the attention. 'She's on her lunch-break.'

'In that case, I can talk to her on the way down to Emergency. All right, Dr Lane?' he said, looking speculatively at Titia. To her ears, there seemed a slight reserve in his tone.

'Mmm.' She nodded, hoping that Rita would not notice that reserve. 'Although I haven't had my usual hasty sandwich yet.'

'You shouldn't admit that in front of Rita here,' he said, taking up a position on the other side of the bed, 'since it's our job to convince her, or bully her, into sticking to a good, nourishing diet. Perhaps we could talk over a salad in the cafeteria.'

'Well…' Titia said, suddenly so acutely aware of those other times when he had bought food for her at the hospital cafeteria that she felt sure he must tune into her thoughts.

'Oh, go on!' Rita encouraged her.

'All right. That would be good.'

When they had taken leave of Rita they talked about her treatment on the way to the cafeteria. 'I've been in touch with the people at the public housing authority about getting Rita into an apartment,' Grant said. 'I made the point that she has a serious chronic illness and can't just be discharged onto the street.'

'Any response?' Titia asked hopefully, matching her

stride to his as they walked along a ground-floor corridor. 'I've been bugging them myself.'

'I think I'm making a breakthrough,' he said. 'They should be getting back to me tomorrow. They've got someone who should be moving out of an apartment any day now.'

'I wish I could do something about that guy who's an epileptic at the clinic, Renfrew Brixton. He has no fixed address, and there's no hope that he could get an apartment in that project because he's an illegal immigrant,' she said, as they passed through the double swing doors of the cafeteria. 'I don't think they would put him on the waiting list.'

'We'll have to ask around the network of private accommodation,' he said. 'Maybe get a room for him. I know a few places.'

They each bought a salad and sat together at a table for two.

'I'm going to watch you to make sure you eat that,' Grant said to her, noting that she glanced at a wall clock nearby.

'I am rushed,' she said, knowing that he was aware of her slight discomfiture with him, the feeling of dissonance. In the years since she had last been in this vast room with him there had been some renovation and redecoration, but it was essentially the same, with its multiple serving areas.

'It's pretty remarkable that we should have met up again after eight years,' he said, looking at her thoughtfully. 'Even more remarkable that you should be a doctor.'

'Yes, perhaps it is.' There was an intensity about him, but she had no idea what he was really thinking.

Five minutes later she stood up to leave. 'Must dash,'

she said. 'Emergency is not quite as laid back as the clinic.'

'Running away again, Titia?' he asked quietly.

'No, I am *not*, Dr Saxby,' she said, irritated.

'No?' He looked cynical. 'Anyway, Dr Lane, don't hesitate to call me if you need an internal medicine consult.'

'I won't,' she said tightly. Everything else aside, he was a very good doctor and she trusted him.

'If that doesn't happen, see you again next Monday at the Open Door,' he said as a parting shot as she was moving away.

Back in the emergency department she threw herself into the fray, welcoming the total absorption that work brought. There would be time later to think more about Grant Saxby.

Soon she was caught up in the challenge and drama of her job, which she loved. One never knew what was going to come through the doors. Every level of one's expertise and training could be used here, every bit of knowledge brought into play. That was the way she liked it.

Having just admitted a patient to the holding area, where he would be observed overnight, Titia went into the triage station, otherwise known as 'the office', where the charts for the new patients were waiting in order of priority. This station was near the entrance, where they could see in all directions, encased by glass in its upper section to keep out as much noise as possible from the near-constant human traffic coming through the entrance. One of the nurses, an RN, greeted her as she went in.

'Hi, Dr Lane.' It was Nancy Wright, RN, one of the very experienced, mature nurses who had come recently from another teaching hospital when the two institutions had merged. Nancy was a great asset to the department.

'Hello, Nancy,' Titia greeted her. 'This is the first time I've had a chance to say anything to you all day. All I've seen of you so far is your back, retreating into the near distance.'

She smiled at the nurse, taking in her dyed blonde hair with its dark roots, cut very short, which contrasted oddly, yet attractively, with her slightly weathered, tired face that reflected the stresses of her job. The ubiquitous stethoscope was stuffed into a capacious breast pocket of her purple scrub suit, as she refused to have it draped around her neck, as some of the staff did. Nancy said it was ostentatious and a mark of the novice. Her age was difficult to determine.

'I've got a case for you here.' Nancy handed her a preliminary chart in a manila folder, attached to a clipboard. 'Could be interesting, and I've got a feeling it's urgent. You know…that sort of gut feeling, based on good old experience?'

'I'll trust your good old experience any day, Nancy,' Titia said.

'It's a sixty-two-year-old guy who's got flu-like symptoms…quite a high fever,' Nancy went on. 'My guess is that he has a rip-roaring infection which could be viral, could be bacterial, or could be caused by some sort of parasite, maybe something exotic. Didn't give a very good history.'

Titia took the folder, glancing at the patient's vital signs and preliminary notes which Nancy had recorded. 'How come?'

'Well, it was only when I was examining his chest that I noticed he had a dark tan on his body, and I asked him if he had got that here or whether he'd been out of the country. He said, yes, he'd been to South Africa. He didn't have any tan on his face,' Nancy said. 'It's amazing how you have to drag things out of some people, that they don't make the connections between things themselves and come up with possible answers.'

'Something he picked up in Africa?' Titia said.

'Could be,' Nancy said. 'Mind you, a lot of doctors and nurses don't put two and two together and come up with four either.'

'True,' Titia agreed. 'I sometimes tend to come up with five, or maybe six!'

Nancy laughed, while she busily punched some data into one of the several computers in the office. 'I think that's better than not coming up with anything, or doing the old "wait and see" bit. Sometimes "wait and see" means staff wait, patient dies.'

'What's your guess, then, Nancy?'

'Well, first of all I thought maybe he had acute food poisoning because he's been vomiting and he's got bad epigastric pain, but then I figured that the swinging high fever doesn't really go with that—it's not right. I reckon he's picked up something exotic from over the water,' the nurse said prophetically. 'Mind you, it could be AIDS, picked up from good old Gresham, with something else superimposed.'

Titia grinned at her. 'Life would be less enjoyable here without you, Nancy. I'll keep in mind what you say. Is there any real indication that he might have AIDS?'

'Not really…just trying to cover all bases,' Nancy said. 'Go to it, Dr Lane, suss him out. He's not a guy to volunteer much, a bit difficult to handle. He obviously feels rotten, but he's not very forthcoming with the info. He strikes me as a wealthy guy who likes to click his fingers and watch other people come running. His wife's with him—she was the one who made him come in, apparently. She seems much more sensible than he is. He's got more than just ''general malaise'' leading up to influenza. Besides, it's not the flu season yet...please, please, please, God!'

'You'd better get a cup of coffee, Nancy, before you deal with anyone else,' Titia commented. 'You look harassed.'

'Yeah, you said it! Glad I'm not on trauma today—they've had a steady stream of ambulance cases. I just had a kid with a little rubber ball struck up his nose.'

'It would have to be little, wouldn't it?' Titia smiled at the thought.

'Don't you believe it! I've seen some amazing things in here. Anyway, that was enough for me for a bit,' Nancy said. 'I couldn't understand how he could take in enough air to do all the yelling he did!'

'Rather you than me, Nancy,' Titia said. 'One thing I don't like is dealing with little kids who come in here. You can't explain very well what's going on, why they have pain.'

'In that case, I'll spare you the details right now of how we got that ball out,' Nancy said dryly. 'I don't know who was more hysterical, the kid, the mother or the granny.'

'I'm going to quiz you later on that. Right now, I'll see what I can make of this one,' Titia said, checking the pockets of her lab coat to make sure she had the essentials for a basic examination—her stethoscope, her penlight for shining in patients' eyes and in their mouths, her ophthalmoscope for a closer look at the eyes, an auroscope for looking in the ears and her computerized thermometer for taking temperatures via the ears, a post-AIDS gadget.

'That guy's in cubicle six,' Nancy said. 'I thought maybe we should call one of the medical staff guys to take a look at him. What do you think?'

'I'll let you know what I come up with,' Titia said, finishing her perusal of the preliminary notes. 'Um… maybe you could put in a call for Dr Grant Saxby anyway, Nancy, before you take off for that coffee. See if he's available. I'd like to get him if I can.' Perversely, she found that she wanted to see Grant, that she could not dismiss him in the way she felt she ought to. So she told herself that her urge to make contact was purely professional, that she wasn't sure that she even liked him all that much as a person, that she would reserve her judgement on that score.

'Sure,' Nancy said. 'Good luck. I'll get Maralyn to take over from me here.' Another RN, Maralyn Tate, was assigned to the triage station and the ambulatory cases for the day, with Nancy. 'If you need anything, Dr Lane, you just shout for her.'

'Will do.'

The man who lay on the examination table, propped up by pillows, in cubicle six was obviously ill. He had that slightly sunken look of the unwell. As Titia entered the tiny room and closed the door behind her, she experienced a sense of shock, followed by a certain sense of foreboding, as she saw the patient staring with bright, glassy eyes at the opposite wall, his face waxy. The nurse had been right. Certainly, at first glance, this looked more than a case of food poisoning or influenza.

A tall woman stood beside the table, although there was a chair on which she could have sat. She was one of those bony, angular women who never seemed to really age, of an aristocratic bearing, intelligent-looking, sophisticated. Her iron-grey hair was styled in a short, wavy, classic look, her clothes of high quality classic style also.

'Ah,' the woman said, with a tone of relief that suggested she had grown tired of waiting, somewhat fearfully, for some sort of verdict on her husband. 'Are you the doctor?'

'Yes, I'm Dr Lane, one of the unit residents. I'm going to examine your husband, then I'm having him seen by someone from the department of internal medicine—Dr Saxby.'

'Good,' the man interjected in an imperious tone. 'We've waited long enough.' To Titia's attuned ear, his speech seemed very slightly slurred. 'I said to Daphne we should have got someone to come to the house. All this waiting is so tiring...I'm absolutely sick of it.'

'You know, dear, that not many doctors make house calls any more, and we had to come here anyway,' the wife said, giving Titia a veiled look of sympathetic resignation. Obviously she was effective and firm in dealing with him, had most likely done it for many years, yet she had realized that he was a sick man, that it was not trivial. 'We need to be here for tests and things.'

'What tests?' her husband asked petulantly. Titia suspected that he was frightened and was being bluff and antagonistic to hide it.

'Blood tests, dear,' his wife said evenly. 'They always want blood tests.'

'Well, Mr. Critchly,' Titia said firmly, 'I'm here to get the ball rolling.' She looked at the note on the clipboard she was holding. 'I see that you've had headaches, nausea, a fever from time to time, muscle pains all over, you've vomited twice and you've had shivering feelings, chills. Now, is there anything else that you want to add?'

'It's the bloody flu,' Mr Critchly said. He was a stocky,

grey-haired man, with a face that, Titia thought, would normally be ruddy. Now he looked waxy and anxious.

'He has pains in his bones as well,' Mrs Critchly cut in calmly.

'The joints?' Titia said.

'No, just the bones in general, and quite severe backache—as well as quite a bad pain across here.' Daphne Critchly made a motion with her hand across her husband's midriff area. 'The nurse here said she doesn't think it's his heart. She said he has a steady pulse, if a bit fast, and his blood pressure is all right. Of course, we were worried about that. Our neighbour, who's a nurse, too, kindly came in to have a look at him at home. She said it wasn't his heart, but we should come in here immediately.'

'And the headaches? Are they severe?' Titia said, writing notes quickly.

'I should say so! Bloody awful. Splitting!' The patient took over from his wife. He seemed to Titia to be one of those men who, when unwell in any way, became rather antagonistic to their wives, as though the wives themselves were personally responsible for the symptoms. They seemed to have a pathological need to have someone to blame…other than themselves. It was an all too common phenomenon.

'Have you had anything to eat or drink in the past twelve hours or so that might have brought this on? Anything at all that you can associate with this?' Titia asked.

'No,' the patient said, folding his arms across his chest in a dismissive way.

'He's been feeling somewhat unwell for about three days,' the wife said patiently, 'then today it suddenly got worse. I took his temperature and it was up, between 103 and 104 on the old scale—we only have one of those old-fashioned thermometers.'

'That's all right.' Titia nodded, making notes swiftly, her mind active. 'I'm going to check it again in a moment. When the nurse took it last time it was only up a little bit.'

'It was like that at home—up and down,' Mrs Critchly said.

'There have been attacks of shivering?' Titia said, getting her equipment for the examination out of her pockets and arranging it on the bedside table.

'Not exactly shivering,' the wife said promptly. 'He's just felt sort of shivery, cold.'

'So nothing that you could call a rigor?'

'Oh, no.'

'I'll want a specimen of your urine, Mr Critchly,' Titia said. 'Have you noticed any change in the colour of your urine?'

'Well…it has been a bit darker than usual,' the patient said grudgingly, a note of apprehension in his tone.

Titia began the physical examination, asking questions and making notes as she went. The temperature had spiked up again. She was gradually putting two and two together and coming up with four.

'When were you in South Africa?' she said, straightening up after feeling the patient's tender midriff area, noting that her gentle palpation of both his liver and his spleen had elicited a response in him that indicated pain in that region. 'Did you take anti-malaria medication?'

'No, we didn't,' the patient said. 'We didn't think it necessary. There's no malaria in South Africa. It's a pretty civilized place, you know.'

'We did use plenty of insect repellent, though,' his wife said. 'We didn't take any chances.'

'Did you go to any other African countries while you were there?' Titia persisted.

'No!' the patient said belligerently. 'Well...'

'We did cross over into Namibia,' the wife cut in quickly, 'but only for two days, and we were very careful with the insect repellent.'

'You should have been taking anti-malaria drugs,' Titia said firmly, not allowing herself to be flustered by this rather superior-sounding couple. 'Your doctor should have advised you about that before you went.'

'Oh, he did—' Daphne Critchly began.

'The side effects of those drugs are bloody awful,' her husband said. 'I've had them before. I knew we would be all right in South Africa.'

'But you went to Namibia,' Titia pointed out.

At that juncture, Maralyn Tate put her head around the door of cubicle six. 'Dr Saxby's here,' she said. 'Shall I send him in?'

'Yes, please,' Titia said. 'And could you get the haematology tech to come up here right away to take some blood. Just a second...'

Quickly she wrote '? malaria' on a piece of paper and handed it to the nurse. 'Tell that to the tech, and Dr Saxby, too.'

The nurse looked at it and raised her eyebrows slightly. 'OK,' she said.

Maralyn flattened herself against the doorframe as far as she was able, instead of moving out of the way, when Grant came through the door, so that Titia could not help noticing that they made physical contact and exchanged glances as they passed each other. Then Grant put a hand on Maralyn's shoulder. 'Thanks, Maralyn,' he murmured.

'Take a look at this Dr Saxby,' Maralyn said, showing Grant the piece of paper. While he showed no reaction at reading the word 'malaria', Titia looked at them stonily as Grant bent his head close to Maralyn's, so that they were almost touching, and left his hand resting on her shoulder.

Titia looked away quickly experiencing an odd feeling of surprise, although she should not have as Maralyn was a very attractive woman. Maybe, Titia reflected briefly, she was one of the three or four women to whom Grant had alluded. Anyway, it was nothing to do with her…

It was good to see Grant, she had to admit as she shuffled papers. She had asked for him, after all, when several other consulting doctors had come to mind also. Titia smiled her welcome involuntarily, albeit a tight smile, when he moved to join them in the cramped cubicle. The pockets of his lab coat were stuffed with a similar array of gadgets to those she carried herself.

'Dr Saxby, this is Mr Critchly.' She made the introduction. 'And Mrs Critchly. Thank you for coming at such short notice.'

Grant nodded and smiled a welcome, only a very slight, rueful gleam in his eyes as he looked at her. 'Glad to be of service, Dr Lane,' he said softly to her, before turning his full attention to the patient and his wife.

'I'm from the department of internal medical,' he explained to them. As he quickly read the notes Titia had made, both the patient and his wife were silent, as though something of the possible seriousness of the husband's illness had penetrated their understanding.

Then Grant asked a few questions of his own and palpated the patient's abdomen, pressing his fingers into soft tissue over the area of the liver. 'Does that hurt?' he asked.

Mr Critchly grunted. 'It sure does,' he said.

As she stood by, Titia went over in her mind what she

knew about malaria. There had been a number of deaths that year in Canada, far too many, among people who had visited tropical countries where malaria was endemic. Some of those people had not taken anti-malaria drugs as a preventative measure or they had been to an area where the mosquitos that transmitted the disease carried a variety of malaria that was resistant to chloroquine, the drug that had been used to prevent malaria for years. In many of those cases the correct diagnosis had not been made by the doctors who had encountered the patients on their return home. Malaria could be treated if it was diagnosed in time.

Titia swallowed her apprehension, hoping for the patient's sake that she was wrong. Malaria was caused by a parasite, sporazoa of the genus *Plasmodium*. That much she remembered from her medical school days. There were several species that affected humans, the most deadly being *P. falciparum*. Once in the human body, the parasite took up residence in the liver and in the red blood cells of the host, affecting the cells' ability to carry oxygen in the haemoglobin, then eventually destroying those cells. The patient's liver and spleen became damaged by the developing parasites and clogged with the products of broken-down red blood cells. Severe anaemia ensued and the patient's tissues became deprived of the oxygen necessary for life.

'We're going to take some blood for tests,' she heard Grant say, 'for a haemoglobin, liver-function tests, blood sugar and blood gases...and for the malaria parasite.'

'Malaria!' Both husband and wife uttered the word in unison, a look of horror passing over their features, as though Titia had not already raised the possibility. Now it had become a probability.

There was a moment of fearful silence.

'I'm afraid so,' Grant said. 'It can be treated. We've found it in time…if it *is* that.'

While the patient seemed shocked into silence, the wife sat down weakly beside him. 'Is it possible?' she whispered.

'Yes, it's quite possible,' Grant said. 'And since you were with him, Mrs Critchly, I would like to get you checked out, too.'

'Oh, my God…' she said.

'As well as the blood samples, I'll want a urine sample from both of you. Sometimes the kidneys are affected. This is a disease that attacks the red blood cells,' Grant explained.

'Oh, my God,' Daphne Critchly said again. 'Malaria…'

'The deciding factor,' Titia explained, 'is the presence of the developing parasites in the bloodstream. We can confirm that easily by taking some blood smears—putting some blood on a microscopic slide, staining it with a specific stain, then looking at it under a microscope. The parasite will be visible. Of course, the microbiologists in the lab here will do that.'

'In the meantime,' Grant said, 'we'll start some intravenous fluids and have the anti-malaria drugs on hand while we wait for that diagnosis. If it's a chloroquine-resistant variety, we use quinine plus tetracycline.'

'That's all I need,' Robert Critchly said resignedly, closing his eyes and putting his head back wearily against the pillows.

'An alternative drug,' Grant explained, 'is something called pyrimethamine-sulfadoxine, which is given with quinine. Then we give acetaminophen to lower the fever. We sometimes need to give a blood transfusion if there's severe anaemia. I hope that won't be necessary.'

'If…if I'm positive,' Daphne Critchly said tentatively, 'will I have to take those drugs, too?'

'Yes,' Grant said.

As though on cue, the haematology tech, a middle-aged Filipino man of imperturbable demeanour, with the unlikely name of Harry, came into the cubicle. With him was the plastic trug he always carried, containing the different types of test tubes with coloured stoppers, syringes, hypodermic needles and lab request forms he required for his job. 'Hi, there,' he said, his eyes darting swiftly to his patients while he grinned a welcome to all occupants of the room. 'I understand you want some stat blood smears, Dr Lane, as well as the usual blood work. Right?'

'Yes, that's right,' Titia said. 'This is Mr Critchly. We also need to test Mrs Critchly.'

'Right,' Harry said, efficiently unpacking the tubes and syringes he would need, together with some glass microscopic slides. 'We can look at these slides right away.'

'We'll need a blood typing and cross-matching,' Grant said, 'just to be on the safe side.'

'OK,' Harry said.

Maralyn Tate came back into the tiny room which was already tight with people. She was a tall, busty, statuesque brunette, with the face of a movie star. Her full, shapely mouth was always painted a bright red. With her wafted the scent of a trendy, expensive perfume. 'Well, Dr Lane,' she said, squeezing past Grant—taking her time about it—to get to Titia, 'anything I can do for you?'

'We need to put up an IV, stat,' Titia said. 'Dextrose-saline.'

'As luck would have it,' Maralyn said, 'the IV nurse is in the department so she can do it. She can put in an

IV in about three seconds so why let a doctor mess about, trying to get it in? Or me, for that matter. OK?'

'Sure.' Titia grinned. 'Ask her to come in.'

'Maralyn,' Grant said, turning his considerable charm on the nurse, 'would you ask Dr Wiess if he could come up here to see a patient? Possible malaria.' As he spoke, he placed his hand casually on the nurse's bare forearm and ran his fingers very lightly down her arm to her hand, before moving his away. It was a gesture that might have seemed inconsequential to any other observer, but to Titia's oddly heightened awareness where he was concerned, it assumed an intimacy that, she told herself, was most likely not intended. She pursed her lips and looked down at the papers she was signing, disturbed in a way she could not understand. It was as though she felt, deep down, that she somehow had a hold on him herself...

The nurse frowned. 'Dr Wiess? Is that the tropical medicine guy?'

'Yes,' Grant said. 'He has his office next to Outpatients.'

'OK. I'll call him right away,' Maralyn said, going out.

'Harry,' Grant said, 'I want those blood smears stained with Giemsa. Tell the guys in the lab. I've got the requisition forms here.' As he spoke, he was filling in several forms for the lab to cover all the tests that they required. 'Make them all stat, would you? We'll be transferring Mr Critchly to a side ward in General Medicine.'

'Right, Dr Saxby,' Harry said, busy with his test tubes and syringes. He already had a needle in a vein and was drawing blood.

'Maybe we'll need more tests after Dr Wiess has seen the patient,' Grant said.

Later, after Mr Critchly had been transferred to a single

room, under the care of the internal medicine department, Titia took a telephone call from Grant in the emergency triage station.

'The call's for you, Dr Lane,' Nancy Wright said, handing her the receiver. 'It's Dr Saxby.'

'Thanks. Maybe he's got the results of those blood smears. Hello?'

'Hi, Titia. I'm afraid those peripheral blood smears on that guy were positive. He definitely has malaria,' Grant said evenly.

'Oh, hell,' Titia groaned. Looking at Nancy, she covered the receiver and said, 'Those blood smears for malaria are positive.'

Nancy rolled her eyes and nodded. 'Not surprised,' she said.

'Will he be OK, do you think?' Titia asked Grant.

'I think so. We got him just in time. There may be some liver damage. Dr Wiess will take over from here. One good thing, his wife is not positive.'

'Good. Imagine going to Africa and not taking anti-malaria drugs,' she commented.

'I guess they thought they would be OK. There isn't endemic malaria where they were for most of the time,' Grant said.

'Hmm…still…' Titia paused, finding herself reluctant to break contact with him. They had not seen each other for eight years before this week; now, perversely, she found that she wanted to be in touch, even though she had told him they should confine their interaction to work. Yet at the same time she did not want to get involved. Feelings that one thought were buried could easily come to the surface where men were concerned. 'Have they got him on the IV drugs?'

'Yes. They started those before they got the results,'

he said. 'And they may transfuse him, just to be on the safe side.'

'Good. Hopefully he'll be OK.'

'Well done, Dr Lane, for making the diagnosis based on the clinical picture,' he complimented her. 'I'm impressed.'

'Well,' she said, trying to resist his attraction, even from a distance, yet hearing the smile in her own voice, 'it was the nurse, really, who suggested it. Nancy.' She gave Nancy a wink of professional recognition. Nancy gave the thumbs-up sign.

'Ah…Nancy,' he murmured. 'A great nurse. There's no substitute for a good, experienced registered nurse in the front lines, especially in the emergency triage situation.'

'And just about everywhere else in between,' Titia agreed, thinking also of Maralyn Tate and wondering if there was anything between her and Grant.

'Yes. Maybe you're talking yourself out of a job, Dr Lane.' There was a teasing note behind the slight reserve she detected in his tone.

'Sounds like it, doesn't it?' In spite of her resolve, she found her mood lightening.

At that moment Nancy gave Titia a meaningful look, rolling her eyes a bit. 'He's dishy.' The nurse mouthed the words. That observation from another woman didn't do anything positive for Titia's resolve.

'Well…thanks for letting me know, Dr Saxby,' Titia added, suddenly feeling self-conscious with him. 'See you next week. Goodbye.'

'He's a great guy,' Nancy observed, apropos of nothing in particular—unless she was adept at reading confusion in Titia's body language. 'Maralyn certainly thinks so.'

'Oh? Are they an item, as the saying goes?' Titia said casually.

Nancy laughed. 'Maybe. Maralyn would sure like to be an item where he's concerned, but she's pretty tight-lipped about him. Anyway, she's got the body for it.' Again Nancy chuckled. 'I'm not sure she's got anything else that he might be looking for, but I advised her to go for it. I'm sure he wouldn't be averse to getting his hands on her—a lot of other guys aren't. Strikes me he's a bit of a lonely guy.'

Titia looked at her. 'Lonely?' she said. 'What makes you think that?'

'Oh…just something about him,' Nancy said thoughtfully. 'He likes women, likes to flirt a bit, but I get the impression it's just a cover-up for maybe wanting something more permanent. He doesn't suffer fools gladly, that's for sure, so my guess is he's looking for someone rather special…but in the meantime he takes what's on offer.' Although she didn't quite say it, Nancy implied that Maralyn was probably on offer.

'I'm surprised he isn't married,' Titia murmured.

'He lived with one of the doctors for several years when he worked at Gresham General, my old hospital,' Nancy said. 'Everyone thought they would be together for good. Don't know what happened there. It's a pity…he's such a great guy. Maybe he hasn't met his match yet.'

'Maralyn's certainly very beautiful,' Titia said absently.

'Yeah.' Nancy chuckled knowingly. 'And she sure capitalizes on it. Can't say I blame her. Even Grant Saxby wouldn't say no to that.'

Looking inward at her own motives, Titia knew with clarity, as well as annoyance, that she was jealous.

As she went about her business, she wondered what Grant really thought of her. A young woman with a flawed past could be seen as a bundle of trouble, even though her own aberration from the norm had lasted such a short while, and even though he had worked for years with homeless and other disadvantaged people. He was certainly tolerant and understanding...or at least he had been. Now she detected a cynicism in him that had certainly not tempered his youthful openness before.

From her point of view, work came first and foremost, as it would continue to do for the foreseeable future. Loving her work, that made it easy. It absorbed almost all her thoughts and energies—and that was the way she wanted it for now.

Sighing, with some loose ends to tie up at work, she checked the time by the wall clock. Her insight told her that the problem was probably really with her where Grant Saxby was concerned, that she was projecting a reaction onto him that he might not give. Still, you always hesitated to show yourself in a bad light. Yet now she knew who she was—Dr Laetitia Lane, a doctor good at her job, respected by colleagues, sure of herself professionally. That was her real identity. Lane had been her maternal grandmother's maiden name. It was not something she had just picked at random, she had a right to that name.

She was looking forward to the end of her shift. Not only did her feet ache, it had been an eventful day in one way and another. She was longing for a cool shower and a long, cold drink. Outside, the heat and humidity would be pretty high. Before going home, she would go once more to see Rita. Maybe Rita would not get any other visitors. While there, she would make sure that Rita's daughter had been informed that her mother was in the hospital even though she felt reasonably confident that Rita would have informed her daughter herself—if she had been able to get past the 'husband'.

Considerably later, as she was leaving the hospital to go home, she saw Maralyn Tate going out through the revolving doors of one of the main entrances. The nurse was dressed in light summer clothing, very attractive. Just ahead of her was Grant Saxby. There was no doubt that they were together.

CHAPTER FIVE

TITIA sat in the doctors' lounge, otherwise known as the coffee-room, on Saturday morning, sipping a cup of coffee with her feet up on a low table, her shoes on the floor. Two other residents-in-training were there, both looking through the morning newspapers, taking advantage of a rare lull in work. There was a pleasant smell of freshly brewed coffee in the air, mingling with the scent of hot croissants which had just been taken out of the microwave oven in the mini-kitchen. She had agreed to work that Saturday morning for a colleague.

Doctors came into this room for a quick respite and a snack in those moments when they could get away from the frantic pace that usually pertained in the hospital emergency department. The room was a sanctuary of sorts, sporting a few comforts of home, with a large refrigerator, a coffee-maker and the other basic accoutrements.

Titia sat, savouring her coffee and a croissant. It was difficult to tell whether this break was a lull before the storm or whether this was going to be one of those days when they actually did not have a great deal of work. She didn't have a gut feeling about it one way or the other. Just as well that it was quiet. She was dead tired, running on the usual steady over-supply of body adrenalin that was the doctor's response to the high level of activity, and anticipated activity.

The phone jangled, making her jump. One of the other residents got up languidly to answer it.

'It's for you, Titia,' he said, extending the receiver to her. 'Doesn't sound like a duty call.'

'Great. Thanks.' She smiled, lifting her feet from the low table and slipping them back into her shoes, ready for action. 'Dr Lane speaking.'

'Hi, Titia. This is Grant.' The unexpected voice non-plussed her momentarily. Maybe the malaria patient had taken a turn for the worse. She hadn't called the floor yet to find out how he was doing, since he was no longer her responsibility. Nonetheless, she intended to do a fol-low-up on him.

'Oh…hi…good morning,' she said. 'Are you here in the hospital, too?'

'No, I'm calling from home,' he said. 'I just wanted to let you know that we may have an apartment for Rita Cook.'

'That's great!'

'I've been negotiating with someone at the housing authority for several days,' he went on. 'Apparently there is a place that someone has been moving out of for about two weeks. They've been trying to get him out for a long time; he didn't take care of the place, to put it mildly. I had a call this morning to say that it's finally empty, but in a bit of a mess.'

'That's great,' Titia said again, 'the best news I've had for a few days. How did you manage it?'

'Persistence has a lot to do with it. I was following up on what you started. The snag is that there's no one to clean the place up right now, if we want it in a hurry, which we do. I was wondering if you could come with me this afternoon to have a look at it, see if it's suitable first of all. I'd value your womanly opinion,' he said.

'That's nice to hear,' she said. The deep timbre of his voice sent a frisson of awareness through her, tuning out her surroundings. It was something she found herself fighting. He had a way of getting under her skin, so to speak, the present Grant Saxby mingling with her memories of how he had been as a medical student. 'Then we would have to clean the place up ourselves…right?'

'Looks like it.'

'It's not my first choice for a weekend activity,' Titia admitted. Then there was her stated intention of confining their interaction to work only. So much for that if she agreed. But it *was* great, really great, that there was an apartment available.

'Squeamish about a bit of dirt?' he said, a slight edge to his voice. And as though reading her thoughts, he added, 'I think that would come under the category of work, don't you?'

'Well…not exactly pleasure,' she said, not wanting him to get the idea that she wanted to be with him. 'And, no, I'm not squeamish.'

'It's not my idea of a weekend activity either,' he said bluntly.

For no obvious reason, Titia thought of Maralyn Tate. Some instinct told her that maybe he had had a prior date with 'the body', as Maralyn was sometimes affectionately known, before this offer of the no doubt filthy flat for their needy patient came up.

'It's time to put your money where your mouth is, Dr Lane,' he added.

'I generally do, Dr Saxby,' she said curtly.

'Glad to hear it. I think that if we don't do this ourselves, nobody else will. And if we don't do it right away, we may lose the place. Word will get around among those on the waiting list, if it hasn't already, that there's an apartment going. I don't want to get Rita's hopes up if it's really run-down. She'll be in no condition to do a major clean-up herself when she gets discharged from hospital,' he said.

'I know that,' she agreed, having the very distinct impression that he was testing her in more ways than one. 'Where is it?'

'That place called Cedar Glen, not far from the Open Door,' he said, describing a small apartment building in the complex of public housing that she was somewhat familiar with.

'I do know the place,' she said. 'I've made one or two home visits to patients there.'

'Right. Could you come?'

'Yes, OK,' she said, stifling a lingering reluctance which was mingled with a recalcitrant desire to see him again, not to have to wait till Monday and the Open Door. 'That's really great that you got it. Sorry if I sounded grumpy.'

'You do sound grumpy.'

'I haven't really got anything important to do…except laundry, cleaning, grocery shopping and all that sort of essential stuff. I guess I can leave it for another week,' she said wryly.

'I think Rita's need is greater at the moment,' he said.

'Oh, sure,' Titia agreed. 'We must go.'

'Hmm. In case it's not suitable, I don't want to tell Rita until we've had a look at it,' he said. 'And to make it up to you, I'll cook dinner for you later…if you want to come to my place. How's that for a trade-off?'

An unaccountable warning of sexual danger, of the pleasurable kind, assailed her momentarily. This was against all the hasty rules she had so recently made for herself, as well as some of the longer-term ones about not getting involved.

'All right,' she found herself saying. 'How about if I

meet you at the Open Door at, say two o'clock? We could go over to Cedar Glen from there. There are shops nearby, we could buy some cleaning stuff.' Already she was feeling much more enthusiastic. 'It's always much more fun cleaning someone else's place rather than your own.'

'Yeah, you know you don't have to do it too often.' Grant laughed. 'See you at two, then—unless I hear from you otherwise.'

'Right. Oh…how's Mr Critchly, by the way? The malaria guy?' she asked.

'He's doing all right. I called the resident covering Dr Wiess's patients this morning. There's an improvement since yesterday, his temp has come down. Its the chloroquine-resistant type, by the way,' Grant said. 'And the falciparum variety, too.'

'I thought it might be both of those things,' she said. 'From now on I'll be asking a lot more patients if they've been out of the country, to South America, Africa and Asia.'

'The resident working with Dr Wiess thinks it's great to have a malaria patient. He's spending a lot of time up there on the floor, and he's thinking of writing a paper about the case for one of the medical journals,' Grant said.

'I hope he does it. Maybe it will help more doctors to be aware of the possibility of malaria, to at least ask patients if they've been out of the country lately when they present with those symptoms,' she said. 'Must go now.'

'Bye for now,' he said.

Titia rinsed her cup at the sink and began gearing herself up mentally to return to the firing line, as it were. Thinking about Mr Critchly, she remembered a line from her medical textbook on malaria: 'Untreated falciparum malaria is frequently fatal,' it had said. It looked as though they had got Mr Critchly in time. By focussing on Mr Critchly she did not have to think too much about Grant Saxby for now.

Things got quite busy after that and when it was clear that she was going to be late meeting Grant at the Open Door she called the clinic from the triage station in Emergency. Esther answered the phone and said she would find Grant, who was hanging about in the Eating Place.

'Hi, Titia.' He was on the line moments later. 'Where the hell are you?'

'Still in Emergency. Sorry, Grant. I'll be leaving here in about ten minutes. Things got hectic here. See you soon.'

'I was beginning to think you'd chickened out. Do you want me to come there to pick you up?' he offered.

'No...no. I'll take the street-car,' she said quickly. 'Thanks, anyway.'

'Sure?'

'Yes.' Before he could say anything else, she hung up.

Cedar Glen was not aptly named. While there were a few trees in the grounds of the apartment complex where Grant parked his car, they were not evergreens. There was an unfenced, open expanse of rather bare, brownish grass that was exposed to the full glare of the relentless summer sun. The trees were dotted here and there on it. There were no flower-beds.

Grant and Titia got slowly out of his car which he had brought to a halt near the entrance door to one of several four-storey buildings. They looked around them criti-cally. The buildings were pleasant enough, Titia thought, if utilitarian. There was no litter spread around on the grass or on the concrete paths that intersected it.

'Well,' Grant said, passing a hand through his thick hair, then wiping the sweat from his upper lip as they stood together, 'it looks reasonably well maintained and clean. At least, from the outside.'

'Mmm.' They stood, squinting against the sun.

'The janitor who gave me the key told me that the previous occupant of the apartment we're going to look at couldn't keep it clean. They've been trying to get him to move for a long time, so I hope you're prepared for the mess I warned you about earlier.'

'He's moved where?' Titia said. 'There's a certain irony in that, as these places are for people who can't afford private accommodation.'

'Don't worry,' Grant said. 'They got him into a permanent hostel where he'll get taken care of, his meals cooked for him, have his own room.'

On the way there, they had stopped at a supermarket and bought some cleaning materials, mops and buckets. Both of them were dressed in shorts and T-shirts. Titia had not seen Grant looking this casual before and she found herself looking with interest at his firm torso outlined under the thin cotton, at his muscled arms. She had not thought of him as muscular, but he was. Certainly he was very fit.

'I hope you're ready for a bit of work of a different sort, Dr Lane,' he said teasingly, turning to her and appraising her in the way she had appraised him. 'Come on, let's haul the gear out. Might as well get the first shock over with. You know, we might find that we actually enjoy this.'

Titia gave a noncommittal murmur. If he felt a lack of ease with her, as she did with him, he did not show it at that moment. The memory of how he had touched her lips with his own nagged at her as she contemplated the job ahead of them, wondering how she was going to get through the next few hours without betraying to him the growing, reluctant, sexual attraction.

'It will be a change,' Titia said, helping him to lift the cardboard boxes of detergents and cleaning materials from the trunk of the car. 'I just hope it's going to be OK for Rita. Maybe we'll have to do a bit of painting as well.'

'It's on the third floor,' Grant said, as he propped open the side door of the building with a convenient brick so that they could carry the stuff through. 'In this heat, I think we'll take the elevator, don't you?'

'Sure,' Titia said, lugging a box, a bucket and a mop. 'It sounds as though you're actually looking forward to it, Grant.'

'I am.' He grinned at her, obviously entering into the spirit of the task, as they walked down a narrow ground-floor corridor to find the elevators. Once again Titia acknowledged how attractive he was, and wondered why he wasn't married.

The smell was the first thing that hit them when they opened the unlocked door to the apartment on the third floor—that and the heat. A wave of it hit them as they advanced through the entrance.

'Hell!' Grant said, going ahead of her.

'Holy cow!' Titia said. 'No air-conditioning!' She laughed as they deposited their loads in the middle of the floor of the living room-cum-dining area and looked around them. 'The windows are all shut, too.'

'It might be worse if they were open,' Grant said. 'What do you reckon that smell is?'

'An eclectic mixture of a wide variety of food stuffs,'

Titia declared ponderously, 'in the last stages of putre-faction.'

'I couldn't have made a better diagnosis myself,' Grant said. 'We've got to get rid of that, you know. Pronto. Otherwise we'll have trouble breathing.'

'You lead on to the kitchen, then.' Titia grinned, know-ing she was, after all, going to enjoy this strange interlude with Grant. 'I assume that the main source of the odour is there.'

'There could be a dead rat or two here and there,' he offered.

'So long as they're dead, I don't care,' she said.

The one-bedroomed apartment had been cleared of fur-niture and carpets, revealing a rather attractive wood floor that could do with a good scrub. The walls had once been white. Now they were blotched where things had been stuck onto them with sticky tape, marked where furniture had rubbed the paint off, mottled with dirty fingermarks.

'This is the pièce de résistance,' Grant said as they stood in the kitchen to survey the mess.

Titia let out a deep breath, saying nothing, as she stood with her hands on her hips, looking at one or two of the cupboards that had been flung open to reveal odds and ends of decaying food which had been left behind. An old refrigerator had its door partly open as well, and the worst of the smell was coming from that.

'The question is,' Titia said at last, 'is this place going to be suitable for Rita?'

'The size and layout's good. The janitor,' Grant said, 'apologized profusely for not having got around to doing more here. The occupant finally moved out this morning.'

'I suggest we get started, then,' Titia said, panting slightly, trying not to take deep breaths. 'Keep the image of Rita in your mind.'

'Yeah,' he said. 'I think we'll risk opening a few windows.'

For about an hour and a half they worked steadily. While Titia cleaned the bedroom and the built-in closet, then started on the filthy bathroom, sloshing pine-scented detergent liberally on everything, Grant worked on the kitchen.

'Hey, Titia,' he called to her. 'Have a look at this place now. And come and have an ice-cold Coke.'

'OK,' she called back. Easing off her thick rubber cleaning gloves, she washed her hands in the sink.

They had opened some windows and turned on two fans which the janitor had left for them. The odour was certainly taking on a more acceptable turn.

'Wow…you've done wonders,' Titia exclaimed when she saw the kitchen. The fridge was now empty and clean, as were the sink, counter-tops and the overhead cupboards. Several very large plastic garbage bags had been filled with stuff to be thrown out, and were very firmly tied at the tops to hold in the smell. Grant was standing at the sink, washing his hands very vigorously.

'It's certainly looking better,' Grant agreed. 'You know, this is just what we went to medical school for.'

They both laughed, standing easily together in the centre of the filthy vinyl floor which he hadn't got around to cleaning yet.

'One has to be adaptable,' Titia said, pushing her brilliant red hair away from her heated forehead. Her hair tended to get a bit curly in this humid weather so she had secured it in a short ponytail with an elastic band. 'Where's that Coke?'

Grant had brought a Styrofoam cooler containing a variety of cold drinks packed in ice. Now he drew out two cans for them and flipped them open.

'Mmm…wonderful,' Titia said in appreciation. 'Thanks.' As she drank, she walked around the kitchen, opening the cupboards under the counter-tops which had not yet been cleaned. 'This is quite a spacious apartment for one person, but is it suitable for Rita, do you think, Grant? Even when we've finished cleaning it, it will still look sort of run-down.'

'I've come to the conclusion that we'll have to redecorate it,' Grant said with a wry grin, looking about the place with a critical eye. 'She'll never be able to do it herself. Paint will make all the difference.'

'Mmm,' Titia said thoughtfully, opening cupboards. 'We'll have to get at it tomorrow because there's no other time. I've got some curtains I could donate…and what about furniture? I don't know whether she's got any.'

'We can ask around,' Grant said, leaning against a counter, watching her. 'There are always people who want to get rid of quite good stuff.'

Titia was still inspecting the lower cupboards, flinging the doors open with a flourish and leaving them open. When she flung open the one under the sink she recoiled in horror. 'Agh!' she said.

'What is it?' he straightened up.

'Look…cockroaches!' she exclaimed. 'Looks like a whole family of them! If there's anything that makes me shudder, it's a cockroach!'

She straightened up to find that Grant was right beside her, bending down to view the scurrying creatures. The cupboard would have been quite dark until she had flung it open.

'Cockroaches are par for the course,' he said nonchalantly. 'The devil to get rid of, too.'

'We're going to get rid of every single one of those,' she said emphatically, 'before Rita sets foot in here.'

'Yeah. They don't do you any harm,' he said, 'compared with the anopheles mosquito, for instance, that gave our patient malaria.'

Titia shuddered. 'I know,' she said, 'it's just the knowledge that they like places where there's dirt and decay…'

When Grant straightened up, his arm brushed hers. 'Squalor is the word,' he said, looking at her with his astute blue eyes which were tinged with amusement at her horror. 'They like squalor. And that's what we're here to fight, isn't it? And fight on behalf of the people who are forced to live in it, usually through no fault of their own. Those who let themselves go, in full consciousness, able-bodied, are a different story—as far as I'm concerned, they can sink or swim on their own.'

She had once seen him as an idealist. Maybe he still was in some ways… But he was a realist, too. He had acquired a hardness that was perhaps in keeping with his years.

'Don't wax righteous, Grant,' she said, pointing a finger at the cupboard. 'What I want right now is a good anti-cockroach spray.'

When he suddenly grinned down at her, a slow lazy grin, Titia felt as though she were melting inside, falling apart. She ought to step back from him, they were almost touching, yet she didn't want him to think that she was recoiling from him prudishly because she wasn't…

Deftly he plucked the empty Coke can from her grasp and placed it by the sink, his own beside it. 'That's something we didn't bring. I can comfort you, if you like, Dr Lane,' he murmured in mock solicitation. 'It's what I'm good at, if you remember…as well as dealing with squalor.' In a moment he had put his hands on her upper arms.

'If you're so good at comforting, how come you're not married?' The words were out, thoughts translated into words before she had known exactly that she intended to say them.

Grant stiffened slightly but did not release his light hold on her as he returned her regard unflinchingly. 'I was as good as married for several years,' he said slowly. 'It didn't work out in the end.'

'Why?' she said. 'You've asked me about myself— you know a lot about that episode from my past—but you don't say much about yourself. You're a mystery.'

'She was in my class at medical school. We decided to live together when we finally graduated.' He shrugged, that slightly bitter twist distorting his mouth. 'It worked for a while, then we somehow grew apart. Maybe we were too familiar with each other. The initial spark that had been there between us sort of flared up and then went out for good, you might say.'

'You seem bitter,' Titia commented, looking up at him, trying to tune out the feel of his hands on her bare arms. 'I don't think you would be bitter if it had just fizzled out.'

'You're quite right,' he admitted. 'She initiated it. Maybe that's what rankles, still. I can't say that I mind now.'

'Was she the only one?'

'Oh, no…there was one other.' The tone of his voice told Titia, sensitive to nuance, that this one had probably been the most devastating of the two.

'What happened there?'

'The usual story. Too much work, not enough play,' he said matter-of-factly.

'And since then it's been safety in numbers?' she persisted, goaded on by an inexplicable need to know and her simmering annoyance from earlier in the week when he had practically forced her to admit that she was the 'runaway girl'.

'Yes. I prefer it that way,' he said. 'That's the way it's going to stay, for a good long time.'

'So do I,' she said, 'but I don't particularly want to be included in that number. Or am I flattering myself just because you have a grip on me?'

Grant smiled wryly and did not answer immediately. In a moment his arms were around her, pulling her against him. Then his hand was under her chin, tilting her face up to him. For a long moment he looked at her. 'You're not flattering yourself,' he said huskily. 'You've turned into a beautiful woman, Titia. I suspect that you could be a charming one, too, if you'd let yourself be. But I suspect that I *do* flatter myself…hmm?'

'I…' Then she in turn was silent. Things had taken a strange turn quite suddenly, almost as though the past had caught up with the present, that they were moving on from where they had left off. The feeling created a dissonance in her that she didn't know how to deal with.

The thought came to her that when she had been sixteen he had kissed her on the forehead, quickly, softly, or on the cheek. Now she was a woman she sensed with certainty that the kiss she knew was coming would be very different. Stiffening, she resisted her own wild anticipation of his mouth on hers as he slowly bent his head down to hers.

At that first, intimate touch she felt a stab of pleasure so acute that she abandoned all thoughts of resistance. Or, more accurately, they abandoned her. Very deliberately, sensuously, he dominated her mouth with his. Yet he was not aggressive or demanding; there was an unselfconscious manliness in him that complemented the womanliness in her. There were men, she mused, who made you feel more intensely female, made you like what you inherently were. Then there were men who made you feel that being a woman was a liability—she had met some of the latter. As Grant's kiss softened, as he tenderly explored her lips with his, Titia knew that he was of the former variety.

Before she could stop herself her fingers were in his hair and she felt his hands slide up her back under the loose T-shirt, caressing her bare skin which was already tingly with heat. With eyes closed, she gave herself up to the pure sensual pleasure of his kiss and his touch. It was as she had known it would be…totally devastating. But she shouldn't be doing this…

'Aren't you glad I washed my hands,' he murmured in her ear when he broke contact, gently biting her earlobe.

In reply, she smiled helplessly.

At last they pulled apart, looking at each other. Grant's eyes were dark with unabashed desire for her, mixed with an expression she could not quite read—a kind of veiled self-mockery. Such a potent combination she had never seen in the eyes of a man before. Or, if she had seen it, she had chosen not to recognize it. Now its message was unmistakable and it totally disarmed her.

'I…I don't think we ought to be doing this,' she whispered as she stepped back from him. There was a vibrant tension between them now as they looked at each other, so that Titia had a startling inner vision of the two of them slowly undressing, lying on the newly washed floor of the empty bedroom and making love, their skin slick with sweat and heat as they came together… Her lips parted in anticipation as the fantasy, then the possibility of a reality, gripped her.

'You're probably right,' he said.

She froze. Out of the corner of her eye she saw a movement. Walking delicately along behind the taps at the sink was the most enormous cockroach she had ever seen. Immediately, she recoiled. 'Oh! Oh!' she exclaimed again. 'There, look!' She pointed. 'That must be the granddaddy of all cockroaches.'

Grant's eyes followed her pointing finger. He did not immediately react. The desire between them seemed to hang in the air, hot and heavy like the atmosphere in which they stood. It was not dissipated as they forced their minds back to the mundane job in hand.

'Grant,' she demanded, 'do something, before it escapes and lives to sire another thousand offspring.'

Smiling, he watched as the creature gingerly ventured out onto the counter-top in full view, a counter that had so recently been scrubbed down with detergent and finally wiped over with a solution of chlorine bleach. 'Why me, Dr Lane?' he asked. 'This is the era of female emancipation, equality and all that. How come I get to pick up cockroaches? Hmm?'

'Well…you're probably much better at it than I am,' she said, backing away from the sink.

'Oh, yeah?' He untied one of the large garbage bags and took out a newspaper and a jar with a metal lid, which had a couple of inches of some indefinable solid stuck to the bottom of it.

'Quickly,' she urged.

'If I'd known you had such a pathological fear of cockroaches,' he murmured, raising an eyebrow at her, 'I might have thought up some way of capitalizing on it…' He left that particular line of thought unfinished as he advanced on the creature, which seemed to be mesmerized into immobility, and placed the upturned jar over it. Then he slid two sheets of newspaper under the opening, trapping the cockroach inside, before flipping the jar upright and securing the lid.

'*Voilà!*' he said. 'It will be quite at home in there. We'll take it on a trip and release it somewhere, rather than flush it down the toilet. I don't like killing things so we'll let it take its chances in the big outdoors.'

'Right,' she said, her lips curving as her sense of the ridiculous increased.

He squinted at the label on the jar. '"Luigi's Extra Zesty Spaghetti Sauce"—that's what it says. Maybe that's its habitual diet.'

They looked at each other. Simultaneously they began to laugh. In moments they were helpless with mirth, leaning against the counter where the hapless cockroach resided in its new home. Tears ran unheeded down Titia's cheeks as she gave way to the rather bizarre humour of their situation, coupled with an abject relief that she could laugh and to the unsought pleasure that she found in Grant's company. The sight of him laughing with her fuelled her own letting-go.

When finally their laughter spluttered to a halt and they stood breathlessly, looking at each other, Titia knew that something had changed between them. There had somehow been a tacit agreement, though she was unsure what it was exactly. Tensely, she waited for something to happen...in the certain knowledge that something would happen.

Grant moved the few paces to reach her. 'Come here,' he said thickly, drawing her against him.

Hungrily they kissed, matching each other in their need, no longer mindful of anything else. Their bare legs touched and she could feel the heat of his body through the thin material of his T-shirt. This was inevitable, Titia thought as she found herself responding blindly to the sensations his searching mouth aroused in her. It was ordained…

Eventually the place was cleaned. They had gone back to work hurriedly, bringing the interlude to an abrupt halt by mutual consent, leaving behind a tension best veiled in work. Both had a sense, largely unspoken, that their coming together was premature. They had finished the living room together, washing the wooden floor with mops and then putting on a self-polishing wax.

'Shall we buy paint this evening?' Titia said to Grant.

'Sure,' he said.

They would split the costs between them, as they had done with the cleaning materials.

The atmosphere between them had changed to one of heightened sexual awareness; it seemed to crackle between them, together with the warm memory of their shared laughter. It was an exhilarating feeling, yet Titia had the warning sense that it was a mistake to get involved too early with this intense man. Her instinct told her that he was not a person to be taken lightly; to get involved with him was to be very serious, regardless of what he had said about safety in numbers. *She* didn't have the safety of numbers, even if he did.

Neither of them referred to those moments of passion in any way openly while they finished the job, keeping thoughts and feelings dampened down with frenetic activity. It was not something that one could really talk about at this stage. It was like a delicate thing growing between them, something that could easily die, she thought. She was not sure that she wanted anything to grow where he was concerned.

And he had made it clear that he didn't want to get involved, hadn't he? That was just as well, she told herself obsessively, because the last thing she wanted at this stage in her career was to get off track into a heavy affair, or anything else. She had her post-grad residency programme to concentrate on, as well as exams at the end of it all. No, she definitely didn't want too many distractions.

The janitor for that particular building came to see how they were doing, just as Titia spread the last of the wax on the floor. She, the janitor, was a middle-aged woman, a bit over-weight, who was panting from the heat when she came through the door of the apartment which they had left open to allow a through breeze.

'Hi, Dr Saxby,' she called out. 'It's Connie.' She introduced herself to Titia.

'Hi, Connie,' Grant said. 'We've just about finished here. We want to come back tomorrow to paint, if that's all right.'

'That's fine with me. Wow!' the janitor exclaimed in admiration as she moved farther into the apartment. 'You've sure cleared up this place…got rid of that awful smell. You know…' She ambled about, carefully avoiding the wet wax. 'It restores your faith in humanity to see such a transformation. It's great to smell lavender, lemon, pine, and all that great stuff…I could smell it all the way down the corridor.'

'It will look even better painted,' Titia said, warmed by the woman's appreciation.

'It sure will. But it's just great now,' Connie said. 'I want to thank you folks for clearing up this mess. If you hadn't done it, I would have had to do it. Would probably have taken me a week.'

'It's our pleasure,' Titia said.

'You know,' Connie said, 'the man who was in this place wasn't a bad guy, he wasn't really the slob he ap-

pears to be. He was sick and he didn't really let anyone
know that he couldn't cope because he was scared to
death of being turfed out. We have strict regulations now
that a tenant has to be able to keep the place clean, at
the very least. This isn't a hell-hole, it's a decent place.'

'We had sort of decided that was the case,' Titia admitted, as she put the finishing touches to the floor with
the foam mop she was wielding, then paused to wipe
perspiration from her heated face.

'Do you think it's going to be OK for your purposes?'
Connie asked.

'Yes, we think so,' Grant said. He had removed his
T-shirt earlier and his bare torso glistened with sweat.
'We were a bit doubtful at first, but now we think it will
be fine. One thing, have you by any chance got an air-
conditioner that we could put in the bedroom window?'

'I'll see what I can find lying about in the storerooms,'
Connie said.

'Great. We're finished here,' Grant said. 'I just have
to take out those bags of garbage.'

'I'll give you a hand,' Connie said, going into the
kitchen and heaving up two of the bags. Grant followed
her out with three more.

While they were gone, Titia stacked their equipment
in the corridor outside the apartment door, realizing that
in an odd way this activity had been a relaxing interlude.
The last thing she picked up was the cockroach in the
spaghetti sauce jar. Its removal seemed symbolic of the
transformation that was taking place in this apartment
and, she hoped, in the life fortunes of Rita Cook. At the
same time she knew that you were only able to help
people so far, if they wanted to be helped. After that
certain point, it was up to them.

The heat and humidity had declined a little when they

went out to load up Grant's car again, but it was still difficult to tolerate. Fortunately they had parked in the shade, otherwise the car would have been like an oven.

'We'll take this stuff over to my place for now,' Grant said, wedging a mop and bucket into the trunk, 'then later I'll donate the lot to Rita. I guess that would come under the category of putting your money where your mouth is.'

'It would,' Titia agreed.

'Do you want to have a shower at my place as it's closer?' he offered, appraising her flushed and shiny face as they stood together beside his car. 'Then I could make us something to eat. This whole thing has taken longer than I thought it would.'

'Thanks,' she said. 'I'll take you up on that.' Too tired to consider any possible complications, she could only think of the pleasures of a cool shower and some food.

'You must be pretty tired,' he said, 'having put in half a day's work in Emergency. Thanks for coming.' His gaze went over her face, settling on her mouth.

'I... Actually, it's been relaxing in an odd sort of way,' she said with a self-conscious laugh. 'For long moments I forgot about work.' She flushed. 'And not just when you were kissing me either. I think the real high came when I finished cleaning the bathroom.'

He laughed. 'It's been fun,' he said. 'Maybe we should make this a sideline.'

'I suspect that the novelty factor would disappear quite quickly.'

As they drove away, Titia wondered if Grant was thinking what she herself was thinking—that the two of them were much more *simpatico* with each other, in spite of certain tensions, than two people would normally have been who had met for the first time less than a week previously, even though they had worked together. There was a certain delicate familiarity between them at the core of their interaction.

The painting on Sunday went quickly and well. They had bought paint in the early evening of the previous day, after calling Rita in the hospital to find out what colours she liked. Green was the colour that she really liked, she had told them, so with rollers on poles they painted the living room a rich, medium-dark green. The effect was stunning. Not only did the colour immediately make the room appear cooler, it had the effect of transforming the rather utilitarian room into something out of the ordinary.

The bedroom they did in a lighter shade of green, the kitchen and front hall were a pale yellow, the bathroom purple. Painting the woodwork a glossy white, with an oil-based paint, took longer. They had brought stools with them so they sat to paint the skirting-boards, then climbed stepladders, lent by the janitor, to paint doors and window-frames.

There wasn't much talking this time as they worked feverishly to get it all done in one day. As Titia painted, she thought of the meal they had had together at Grant's place the previous evening. Contrary to some of her expectations, he had been very businesslike, cooking them a simple, delicious meal, then driving her home immediately after. Now the transformation of the apartment was almost complete. When the paint was dry, she would hang curtains later in the week.

'Come back to my place,' Grant said, when they had finally come to a satisfying end to their work, 'for something quick to eat and a shower.'

Wearily Titia nodded. 'So long as it's quick,' she agreed. 'I'm exhausted.' There was no premonition of any possible outcome of the seemingly innocuous invitation, only a gentle frisson of anticipation at being in his company in a relaxed setting.

'Hey,' he said, as they were going through the door, carrying the smaller equipment, 'you've got splatters of paint on your nose. You look rather cute, speckled green.'

Titia grinned back at him, but made sure she kept one step ahead. Complications weren't what she needed now—and she had to remember that!

CHAPTER SIX

HAVING seen Grant's apartment on the previous day, Titia knew her way around at least superficially.

'Leave the stuff in the back hall,' Grant said to her as they entered the welcome air-conditioned coolness of his apartment, which took up the entire second floor of a three-storey Victorian house. It was situated on a quiet street, in a 'reclaimed' area, not far from the Open Door Clinic. Gleaming oak floors, open marble fireplaces and plaster cornicing gave the apartment an understated charm and opulence. It contrasted with Titia's own apartment which was in the modern, low-rise block.

They dumped their painting gear in a small back hall where a door opened out to a cast-iron fire escape. 'Would you like a cold drink, Titia?' Grant asked. 'Or maybe tea? We'll get something to eat later, when we've cleaned ourselves up a bit.'

In the confined space of the tiny hall he appeared large, towering above her. His dark hair was moist with sweat, tendrils of it falling over his forehead, while the thin fabric of his T-shirt clung to his muscled torso. With the smell of paint that clung to them, she could also smell the odour of clean sweat as she stood mere inches away from him, mingled with the scent of aftershave that still lingered, it was a heady fragrance, and she allowed herself the pleasure of it, not moving away.

'Um…I think tea would be good.' Her throat was suddenly dry, and not from the heat or from her thirst. 'Thanks.'

Grant reached out and placed a hand gently on the side of her neck, his thumb caressing the angle of her jaw. 'It's been a good day, hasn't it?' he murmured. 'We've accomplished a lot, all we set out to do. Hmm?'

'Yes,' she agreed, having trouble meeting his eyes, 'it *has* been a good day. I'm just pleasantly exhausted. I'll go back there tomorrow after work to make sure the place is aired out, just to do a final check.'

'Great. We'll start asking around for furniture.'

His caressing touch was having an hypnotic effect on her so that she could not move. Almost imperceptibly she swayed towards him.

'Even that granddaddy of a cockroach is probably having a great time,' he teased her. They had released the cockroach under a bush in the park, the bush being near a large garbage can. They had laughed like two kids when the creature had emerged slowly from the jar to view its new surroundings and Grant had tossed the jar into the garbage can.

Now, Titia sensed, the time for childlike fun was over for this particular day. There was a sharp awareness, a very adult tension, between her and Grant, a potent sense of something waiting to happen.

'Tea it is, then. Right?' he said.

'Please,' she said, looking up at him. His eyes were dark and intense, his expression suddenly serious.

'Thank you for a great day,' he said. 'I haven't relaxed so much in a long time.'

'It wasn't my doing,' she said softly. 'There's something very relaxing about painting. Maybe you should have done some of it with those other women who left you.' Although she spoke facetiously, she found that in a very serious way she wanted to know more about him, to fill in the gap of the eight years since she had first set eyes on him, to find out what made him tick.

'We did,' he said. 'But not for homeless people. They were not interested in my…obsession, perhaps I should call it, for working with street people. That's what got in the way each time.'

'Why did you let it?'

'I decided not to compromise my ideals and standards, I guess. I was committed,' he said quietly, thoughtfully, as though he had not really thought it out carefully before. 'A lot of people give up on their commitments when the going gets rough. They don't follow through. You can't be a dilettante in this business. You either don't get in at all, or you stick with it.'

'Yes…I agree,' Titia said, 'but you also have to be flexible, Grant. You have to accommodate the needs of other people, too, the person you are living with.'

'So, runaway girl, you've taken it upon yourself to advise me. That's ironic.'

'Don't call me that,' she said. 'I'm not a girl any more, and I don't want to be constantly reminded of that. I want to move on, Grant, and so should you.'

Grant slid his hand round to the back of her head and drew her towards him as he bent his head down to her. 'Tishy.' He murmured her name just before his lips grazed hers. 'Good idea. Maybe I'll start right now.'

Stiffly at first she stood in the circle of his arms, then her own arms slid round him. For such a long time she had worked hard, studied, not had enough time for something like this with a man. Perhaps it was all catching up with her. Perhaps she had been waiting for Grant Saxby to reappear in her life. Yet there was a sense of not being ready. Was one ever ready? Or did this muted longing, this desire for physical contact, just hit you, just come out of the blue when you were least expecting it?

Now, as she felt the beating of Grant's heart against her own, felt the rise and fall of his chest, she fully realized how starved she was for this kind of male contact. In her everyday work she dealt with plenty of men, colleagues and otherwise. Very few of them moved her in any way other than in the respect she felt for them as colleagues. A precious few of them were friends, nothing more. She felt as though she were waking up from a self-imposed oblivion into a powerful awareness that here was something she might not be able to control.

Grant slid a hand down her back, tracing the indentation of her spine, over the curve of her hips in the thin cotton shorts that she wore, easing her against him. The action was so natural, so sensual, that she allowed herself to move closer against the contours of his body. With her head thrown back for his kiss, it seemed that they had been fashioned perfectly for each other as they moulded their bodies together, as she felt the faster rise and fall of his breathing.

He was the one to draw back from her. They looked at each other in silence as unspoken questions passed between them.

Ruefully she smiled. Those questions might never be asked.

'Tea?' she said prosaically.

'Sure,' he said huskily, laughing at her.

'I don't want to be one of your women, Grant,' she said.

'I don't think I want to make you one,' he said.

Whatever he had meant by that, she was not going to cross-examine him to find out. 'Shall I take my shower first?' she said, with more coolness than she felt.

'Sure, go ahead,' he said.

In the sanctuary of the bathroom she locked him out.

Later, when they were both clean, drinking tea and eating sandwiches, Grant asked her again about the past. 'I'm curious to know why you lied to me,' he said, as they sat in his comfortable sitting room. He had changed into a clean shirt and pants and his hair was slicked back casually with water so that he looked cool and refreshed, while she still wore her T-shirt and shorts.

'I...I'm ashamed of the past,' she said hesitantly, 'ashamed of the way I reacted so that I ended up on the street. It was a stupid thing to do...but at the time I acted instinctively. The loss of my father unhinged me temporarily, so that I made the wrong decision...to put my mother through such anxiety...'

'So you wanted to pretend, when you met me again, that it hadn't happened?' he said.

'No...yes...I don't know. I was just ashamed. We managed to cover it up, I and my mother.' She looked down at her hands which were tightly clenched in her lap. 'It's something that I want to put behind me.'

'Go on,' he said.

'You, of all people, should understand how I felt,' she said, 'and how I feel now.'

'What do you mean—me, of all people?' he demanded quietly.

'Because you deal with people who have things to hide. All they have left is their pride sometimes, a desire for privacy. Anonymity, too, sometimes...' Her voice trailed off as she felt that she wasn't explaining herself very well. The mundane words did not match the angst and regret she felt in her heart.

'I came from a sheltered background,' she added quietly. 'I wasn't tough, in the way that I could go back to my normal life as though nothing had happened. But I *have* managed to put it behind me.'

'I missed you when you left,' he said. 'I also worried like hell about you.' Although there was no censure in his tone, she knew that he had, perhaps, expected her to behave differently at the time.

'I did leave that note. I obviously didn't consider it enough from your point of view,' she admitted. 'I'm sorry.' No, she had not thought then of how he might have felt because she had been concerned with her own feelings and, with regard to the crush she had had on him, she had thought then that he could not possibly have felt anything like that for her in return, because he was older, more sophisticated, more *together*. He had been all the things she had not been at that time. Had he been in love with her? She didn't think so. At the time she hadn't felt lovable.

'You sure didn't consider,' he said evenly.

Titia realized that she was the captive here, that she could not get away from his questioning until she left. His pride had been hurt in the past, that was all. Abruptly she stood up, feeling oddly close to tears. Having thought that she had put all that behind her, it was evident that she had only put some things behind her, that her dormant feelings for Grant had reawakened in some way. Perhaps they would not stand up to the light of day, as it were, would not stand up to adult scrutiny. Right now she did not want to put them to any sort of test.

'I was only sixteen at the time, Grant. *Sixteen.* I'd just had a terrible loss. I appreciate what you did for me, very, very much. But I wasn't thinking about *you*. I was thinking about *myself*.' She spoke vehemently, her face taut. 'I had enough trouble, worrying about myself.'

Slowly he got up, too, to tower above her. 'What's your real name?' he said. 'It sure isn't Patricia Ranley. Is it, in fact, Laetitia Lane?'

'Patricia was my name,' she said. 'Ranley is my paternal grandmother's maiden name. Lane is my maternal grandmother's name. Laetitia Lane is who I am.'

'And your father's name?' he said quietly, staring down at her.

Titia hesitated. 'I stopped using that name a long time ago. I wanted to create an identity for myself that did not have anything to do with those events. Dr Laetitia Lane is who I am. It's who I want to be.'

'My God, if only you knew,' he said.

'Another reason I didn't tell you last Monday when we met is that I thought you would reject me,' she said, staring at him. 'It's quite one thing to help someone when they are in dire need, and quite another to have that person as a colleague, or to have any sort of...any sort of relationship with them.'

'I see,' he said flatly.

'And that's just what you are doing, Grant, isn't it? Rejecting me?' she asked bitterly.

'No,' he said wearily. 'I wish you hadn't lied to me the other day, that's all. I guess I was ninety-five per cent sure that you were Patricia Ranley...or whoever. Then when you flatly denied it, I decided to go with the other five per cent.'

'I...' Her throat felt closed up so that no words would come out.

'I wish, too, you hadn't just disappeared all those years ago,' he said vehemently. 'I do—and did—understand what you were going through, so I wish you could have given me credit for that understanding.'

Titia took a deep breath, looking around her as though

seeking a means of escape. 'I wouldn't have come here, Grant, if I'd suspected that you were going to question me.'

'Are you in denial, Titia, about what happened?'

'No, of course not. I don't want to dwell on it. I had better go,' she said.

'You don't have to,' he said.

'I want to.'

They stood in silence beside the table where the remains of their simple meal was spread out. Then he put a hand on her arm. 'Titia, you don't have to go.'

'Yes, I do,' she said, tears pricking her eyes, somehow having found her voice. 'I'm in an untenable position. What right have you to be angry with me? I thought that the help you gave me had no strings attached. You said so at the time.'

Grant sighed. 'Yes, of course. There were no strings. I'm not angry. But I cared about you.' There was a quiet insistence in his voice, a bitterness.

'And I cared for you.' She whispered the words.

'There was no need to lie,' he insisted.

'For me there was,' she said. 'It's all right in theory to be perfectly honest, but in reality it's not always easy when you have a lot to lose. Your first instinct is to defend yourself. I wanted to create an identity for myself. You said yourself that we're all multi-faceted, that we should choose the part of ourselves that we like the best and develop that. It was your philosophy, Grant, that has sustained me all these years, through medical school. I am now what I want to be. I don't want that self to be threatened.'

There was a silence while he thought about what she had said. 'I remember saying something like that,' he admitted. 'I do understand, but obviously not enough.'

'I'd better go home.'

'I'll drive you home,' he said.

'No! I'll take the street-car,' she said insistently, knowing that in a few minutes she would be in tears if she remained with him. All she knew at that moment was that she was feeling a sharp, poignant sense of disappointment.

'Of course I have to take you home,' he said quietly.

Titia backed away from him, finding herself backed up against a table, where he was able to grasp her upper arms in his warm hands, detaining her. 'Please…we mustn't part like this,' he said.

'Why not? I got the impression that this was what you wanted. Everything neat and tidy, tied up,' she said wildly.

In reply, he kissed her, gently, deeply, until she pushed him away. 'Don't do that.'

'We'll talk about this tomorrow,' he said, 'if you're sure you must go now. I think you're rather mixed up, Titia, if you still feel that you have to lie about yourself.'

'Then you don't understand,' she said. 'Maybe one day I won't feel the need.'

'Where does the name "Laetitia" come from?' he said.

'I saw it in a society magazine,' she said matter-of-factly, staring him full in the face, unflinchingly, 'and decided that I liked it. Then and there I adopted it. I had a very close relationship with my maternal grandmother, whose name was Lane. That is who I am—Laetitia Lane. If you want Patricia Ranley, I'm afraid you're eight years too late.'

With that, she pushed past him and hurried to the door. In seconds she was walking rapidly down the stairs to the first floor, then out the main door to the street, hearing him call her name as she ran.

In the end she could not take a street-car because her eyes were filling persistently with tears. Behind her sunglasses the tears seeped free and she mopped them up as best she could. She walked to her apartment building through small back streets and parks, not that far, really, from where Grant lived.

'What now?' she asked herself as she finally let herself into the sanctuary of her apartment. He had told her that she was mixed up. But she didn't feel particularly mixed up, not any more. Yes, she had lied to him. She had done it instinctively and it was no big deal, she told herself. In any case, he would have found out who she was. She would have to examine her own motives for why she had lied. Maybe she would be dogged by shame all her life.

Wearily she lay down on her bed. All through her walk home she had had a sense that she had somehow let him down. Had she let him down? Perhaps his other relationships had broken down because he, in his idealistic way, had expected too much of them. Maybe he had expected too much of her.

Titia was in her robe when there was a ring on her intercom doorbell in the hallway of her small apartment. As she went to answer it, a sharp premonition made her hesitate as she pressed the button to communicate with whoever was down in the lobby.

'Hello,' she said tentatively.

'It's me…Grant,' his terse voice said. 'I want to talk to you.'

'I don't—'

'Don't send me away,' he said. 'I'm not happy about the way we parted.'

She could hear background noises from the lobby,

sensing that he was keeping his voice low so that he could not be overheard. To avoid giving him unnecessary embarrassment, she gave in. With her, too, there was a restless sense of having left him inappropriately, of having been ungracious of his hospitality.

'Come up,' she said.

In her bedroom she quickly got dressed in a skirt and loose, casual top so that she was ready at the door when Grant knocked.

'I don't want to leave things like this between us,' he said tensely when she had shut the door behind him. 'I think we should talk, put it all behind us, while we're in the mood for talking.'

Titia shrugged. 'All right,' she said. 'Come in. Would you like coffee?'

'Not at the moment, thanks,' he said, moving with her into the sitting room. 'Titia, there's too much unfinished business between us. If we have to work together, as we do, we might as well get it out of the way so that we can get to know each other in the here and now.'

'Why…why does it matter so much?' she said, turning to face him.

'Because I find that it does. I want to get to know you,' he said tersely. 'Isn't that what you want?'

'No…no, I don't…' She struggled to utter the denial, but the lie stuck in her throat.

'Liar,' he said softly.

Nonplussed, she stared back at him, a constriction in her throat. 'I'm going to have coffee, even if you aren't,' she declared, needing a diversionary tactic. While she prepared the coffee he stood in the kitchen doorway, looking at her.

'Talk to me, Titia. Tell me what has happened to you

since I last saw you in my sister's room in the medical residence.'

'I thought I told you that already.' Busily she spooned ground coffee into the coffee-maker and added water.

'I want to hear all of it.'

'I guess I suddenly came to my senses,' she said, with her back to him as she got mugs out of a cupboard, finding now that she almost welcomed getting a few things off her chest. 'It was suddenly over, I was ready to go back.'

'And?'

'There was another reason I decided to do it that way, without telling you ahead of time.' She turned to face him. 'Because I was getting to like you too much...a schoolgirl crush. It was becoming an impossible situation all round. I was grateful to you...I still am. I didn't tell you my real name because I had to be careful. Even though I trusted you, I was just being sensible.'

He raised his eyebrows at her, a self-mocking gesture. 'I'm flattered,' he said.

'I've outgrown that, too,' she said quickly.

He laughed softly. 'I see,' he said, his face shuttered so that she could only guess at what he was thinking. 'And how is your mother?'

'She's fine now. We see each other regularly, we're very close. As I've already said, I was ashamed of that episode in my life. You see, Grant, you don't know what it's *really* like to be homeless, to be in that disadvantaged position. Neither did I until I experienced it. You're tolerant, I know, and you may think you understand, but you don't.' Titia leaned forward to look at him earnestly.

'You don't necessarily have to experience something to have a certain empathy for those who have, otherwise none of us would be able to function,' he said. 'But I know that's not like being there. Go on.'

'You don't know what it's like to have that gut feeling of acute anxiety with you all the time…for your own safety, from not knowing where you'll sleep to where you'll get the next meal. You never have any privacy or any sort of security. That awful anxiety is with you every minute, like a physical sickness… It's there last thing before you go to sleep, it's there the second you wake up in the morning,' Titia said, memories crowding back. 'I don't want to dwell on it.'

'Tell me,' he said. 'I want to know.'

'You know, at that time, among some of my school-friends, it was considered cool or trendy to pretend that you were poor…when you weren't poor.' She struggled to express herself. 'You know, they used to cut holes in their jeans, wear broken-down old shoes with the laces trailing, have holes in their school uniforms. Some of them used to buy donated clothing from places down-town that were set up for destitute people, where you could buy clothes very cheaply by the pound.'

'Yes,' he said quietly.

'They could do it to be cool because they had rich parents to fall back on—or, at least, parents who were pretty well off, who could afford to send them to a private school.' Titia found that her voice was less than even so she stopped to pour herself coffee.

'I'll have some after all,' he said, moving over beside her to pour himself coffee.

'What I found out,' she went on, 'is that there is noth-ing trendy about living on the edge of poverty all the time, wearing someone else's cast-off clothing, worrying about having your shoes stolen if you dare to take them off in a hostel, or having all your belongings stolen. No…

You're on the edge of an awful fear...all the time. And you're ashamed. Yes, you're bloody ashamed! You don't want holes in your jeans, or frayed trouser legs when you *have to* have them. It isn't cool when you *have to* buy all your clothes at jumble sales or at charity shops for the destitute.'

Grant stood silently, looking at her under lowered brows. He had wanted a more detailed explanation from her and he was going to get it, Titia vowed silently. Vaguely aware that she was repeating herself, the words nevertheless came tumbling out of her mouth. Nothing was going to shut her up now until she was well and truly finished.

'That fear wears you down, you know. It eats away at you day after day because there's no respite. Oh, I had money to back me up...but I was scared to get it out of a bank machine too often. I thought I could be traced, and I didn't want to be found...in the early days.'

'Go on, Tishy,' he said. 'I'm listening.'

'What I learned about myself on the street was that I had bought into the myth of "cool". I saw how silly it was. It was a pretence. I found out that it was a mockery of genuine poverty because if you're an ordinary, decent person, fallen upon hard times, you're ashamed of looking scruffy, looking poor. You want to go in the opposite direction, you want to hide it...you want to be ordinary, middle-of-the-road anonymous. It's degrading when you can't keep yourself or your clothes clean.'

Tears were pricking her eyes now as she walked across the small kitchen and turned to face him. His expression was arrested, disturbed, and she was glad. At least she was getting through to him.

'It's such a relief to be ordinary. That's why I lied to you, Grant. I felt shame...as I've already told you,' she said. 'Even though I had just lost my father, even though I was running away from Terry, I felt shame because I knew that I had other options open to me. Don't you understand? It was because of the unwitting mockery I had made of it before I knew what it was really like, because of the lack of real understanding.'

'I think you're making it unnecessarily complex, Titia. We all make a mockery of things in some form or other, almost every day of our lives,' Grant said quietly. 'We do it through innocence and ignorance. You were very young.'

Titia scarcely heard him. She went blundering on, yet becoming more articulate as her thoughts collected themselves and clarified.

'You don't know the first thing about what it's like to go down and not know how to get up,' she said bitterly. 'All the work you're doing…it's under false pretences…' Biting her lip, she stared down at the floor.

'Titia…' Grant said her name softly.

The image of her father came to her mind. 'All those years ago,' she whispered thoughtfully, 'I was so preoccupied with being a runaway that I didn't really mourn enough for my father.' Now it was all with her again, coming back like a flood, like a well of sorrow, to overwhelm her.

They sipped the coffee, standing awkwardly on either side of the tiny kitchen. Most of the time she did not look at him as she wrestled with emotions that had come to the surface.

'So that's what it all means,' she said at length. 'I wish you hadn't forced me to open old wounds. I really had put all that behind me, you know.'

'Had you?' he said quietly.

'I think you should look at yourself, Grant,' she said

astutely. 'Two failed relationships is a lot in someone of your age. Maybe you expect too much of others, and maybe too much of yourself. Maybe you need to be more tolerant of the women in your life…give more to them, instead of to your ideals.'

'What do you know about my private life?' he challenged.

'Not much, admittedly, but I'm good at picking up vibes,' she countered.

'What about you, Titia?' he challenged. 'You're not married, you're not living with anyone. It seems to me that you haven't even tried.'

'I'm not ready to marry anyone.'

Leaving him abruptly, she went into the bathroom to stare at her strained face in the mirror. This was not quite the way she had envisaged the evening, she told herself again, not this giving way. Yet she wasn't embarrassed, as she would probably have thought ahead of time that she would be, had she suspected this might happen.

Taking deep, calming breaths, she assessed herself. A strange sense of peace was coming over her, a deep sense of sobriety, of understanding.

'It's all over,' she said to her reflection. 'It's come to an end at last.' During all those years, when she had thought she had moved on, there had still been a residue of unfinished business.

After a few minutes she washed her face and hands with cold water and combed her hair, her movements slow and deliberate. A rueful sense of something like amusement imposed itself on her calming sobriety. What a lot of angst over something that had to be put in its place, firmly in the past! She remembered the old adage in psychology: you could not change the past, but you could change the way you looked at it. There was a light-

ness in her that had not been there for a long time, as
though an actual physical load had been taken away from
her. By expecting her to give an account, Grant had ef-
fected a catharsis.

When she came out he was standing in her sitting
room, waiting for her. Maybe now he was the one who
needed to expunge the past, the insight came to her...not
so much with her, perhaps, as with his other women.

'Satisfied, Grant?' she asked.

'For now,' he said.

'And what were your motivations, Grant Saxby, back
in those days of idealism?' she said. 'You were certainly
different.'

She had got him there, she could see that, as he
shrugged and thrust his hands into his trouser pockets. 'I
guess I wanted to be the perfect doctor. I wanted to elim-
inate the ills of the world...you know, the white knight,
coming to the rescue.'

'Past tense, I see,' she said.

'Yeah. I guess I've grown up a bit since then, too. Not
given up, though. I'm sorry I allowed my own motivations to get in the way of my full understanding of the
tragedy for you. You see, when you went away and I
couldn't find you, I felt that I'd failed.'

'You didn't fail. Maybe now there can be a sense of
closure,' she said.

Grant came over to her and cupped her cheek with his
hand. Lightly he ran his thumb over her lips, a gesture
that sent a shiver through her so that she closed her eyes
for a few seconds. 'Don't do that,' she whispered, but
she did not move away.

'Closure of the past,' he said, not releasing her. 'But
what about the here and now?'

'I...I don't know,' she said. 'Maybe you should be

more tolerant of the women in your life…not expect them to share your dedication, if one can call it that.'

'I've moved on, too, since then, to a large extent, though maybe not enough. I know there's only so much we can do. We have to accept our limitations, without giving up.'

'Just so,' she agreed. 'Would you…um…like more coffee?'

'No, thanks. Come and sit down. Why are we just standing here?'

She laughed self-consciously. 'I don't know.'

When they were seated on her sofa, she said, 'I didn't so much reinvent myself as emphasize those parts of myself I liked best. I wanted to use my brain and the compassion I felt I had.'

'Maybe I was full of hot air in those days…sound and fury, signifying nothing much…' Grant said, 'or whatever it was that Shakespeare said.'

'No…I appreciated you.'

'We all have to search for identity when we're young… sometimes in later life, too, after we've made a few wrong turns. Congratulations on being an MD, Titia,' he said.

'Thank you,' she said. 'I did come from a loving home after all. For me there was some sort of back-up, for which I'm eternally grateful. I've seen what happens to a lot of the people who have no back-up, who don't have what some psychiatrists call ''an additional self''. My mother was on my side, really, all along. I was able to go to a good school, with teachers who cared about me.'

'I'm glad that was the reality of it,' he said.

'Now I don't even know what ''cool'' means,' she admitted.

When there seemed no more to be said, nothing else

to distract them from their inexorable mutual sexual attraction, she stood up. Grant got up as well, unfolding his tall body from the comfortable sofa, stretching languidly. Sensitive to nuance, Titia suspected that he was not as calm as he looked.

'You'd better go, Grant. It's been a long day and I'm tired.' She said the mundane words, not trusting that she could control her own emotions, knowing that something had happened between them, signifying a new starting point...or an ending.

Grant put his hands on her shoulders and kissed her gently on the mouth before she sensed what he was going to do, a soft exploring kiss, a touch of comfort that seemed to her, in her heightened awareness, to put a final seal on the past.

'Have you ever lived with someone?' he asked. 'A man?'

'No.'

'Will you live with me, Titia...come and live with me?' His face was drawn and tense as his eyes held hers. 'I want you, more than I can say.'

Shocked, her heart leaping with an unexpected anticipation, Titia nonetheless pulled back from him. 'Considering your record with women, Grant,' she said, forcing a calmness, 'I don't think that would be a good idea.'

'I think we would be good together,' he said.

'You mean in bed?' she said, reading him astutely.

'That, among other things,' he said candidly, putting his hands nonchalantly into the pockets of his linen trousers as though, it seemed to her, they were discussing the weather.

Titia swallowed a lump in her throat. 'I...I don't want to be number three, Grant. I don't want to be the next discard. You'd better go now.'

With that, she walked to her front door. 'I'm glad you came,' she said truthfully. 'It's been a very interesting experience.'

At the door he confronted her again. 'Titia,' he said softly, 'come with me. Stay with me tonight…then come and live with me.'

How tempting he was, she thought, her eyes going over him. He was a gorgeous man, who would, no doubt, be a great lover. Her thoughts veered away from that, dwelling only briefly on the uncomfortable certainty that living with him would be pleasurable in the extreme but wrong for her right now. Lifting her head up proudly, choosing deliberately to misunderstand him, she said, 'As I told you earlier, Grant, I'm not ready yet to marry you…or anyone.'

To his credit, he grinned ruefully, his perfect white teeth adding even greater charm to his attractive face so that Titia wondered momentarily how she managed to refrain from throwing herself at his feet. Many other women would have done, she thought, particularly the lovely Maralyn Tate.

'And I guess,' she added, 'that you are not either.'

It was not necessary for him to say anything. The wry gleam in his eyes told her everything as he leaned forward to kiss her farewell. Deliberately she put her arms around his neck and kissed him back, turning what he had probably intended to be a quick kiss into something quite different. With the tip of her tongue she lightly touched his mouth, then deepened the kiss, pressing her body against his until she felt him respond. For a long time they stood like that until his ragged breathing and her own heightened response caused her to draw back before she found herself promising him anything.

At arm's length she looked into his eyes which were

dark with desire for her. 'Try the beautiful Maralyn Tate,' she suggested huskily. 'I'm sure she would be pleased to oblige you.'

There was veiled admiration in the way he looked at her as he tried to control his visible physical response to her. 'You're a witch, Dr Laetitia Lane,' he said slowly. 'It's you I want.'

'We can't always have what we want,' she said. 'Goodnight, Grant.'

Trying not to laugh with a wild sense of triumph, Titia slid to the floor when he had gone, drawing up her knees and putting her head down on her folded arms, breathing evenly to still the pounding of her heart. It seemed incredible that a week ago she had had no hint that he would come back into her life, that she would be working with him, kissing him. It seemed like the hand of fate.

Already, seconds after he had gone, she was missing him. It was tempting to fling open the door and call him back. But she didn't do it. She didn't know how to handle him, or the powerful emotions he evoked in her. It was too soon after putting the past to rest.

As she sat there quietly, to think things through, there was a sense that she was running away from him and from herself.

CHAPTER SEVEN

TITIA was glad that Monday was a clinic day as the pace was more relaxed than in Emergency, yet she had very mixed feelings about working all day with Grant. Arriving early at the clinic, on another hot day, Titia went first to the Eating Place to get herself a cup of coffee. The staff in the kitchen, many of them volunteers, greeted her warmly.

'Hi, there, Titia,' one of the cooks called to her. 'How you doing?'

'Not too bad. It's nice to be back here,' she replied sincerely. Indeed, she would be very sorry when her official stint at the clinic came to an end. Maybe she would put in a few hours as a volunteer, here and there, so that she could keep in touch with some of the regulars that she really liked. They needed to have some continuity in their lives, to see the same people, in a type of existence that gave them little opportunity for continuity.

As she helped herself to freshly brewed coffee, she knew exactly when Grant walked into the room, even though she had her back to the door. Hyper-sensitive to his presence, she sensed rather than saw his approach towards her, and her heart jumped in anticipation.

'Good morning, Titia,' he said softly, as she turned to him. 'How are you?' There was a wealth of meaning in those mundane words.

'All right,' she said. 'How are you?' It seemed absurd that they were talking in this slightly stilted way, but she could not help herself as they seemed to feel their way around each other emotionally, like two cats about to spring.

'Suffering a little from the heat,' he said, helping himself to coffee, 'as well as from a certain lack of sleep.' The hint was unmistakable, and she gained a small, grim satisfaction from it. Yet the satisfaction was tinged with sadness. She found that she wanted him to like her.

Today he wore thin cotton pants in a stone colour and a cream-coloured cotton shirt, with the long sleeves rolled up. He looked cool and sophisticated, and—she had to admit it—very attractive.

'Lack of sleep?' she queried, forcing a lightness to her tone. She felt weighed down by the possibility that he was burdened by having known her in the past, for having tried to help her.

'A lot on my mind,' he said, turning to give her a long, appraising glance, taking in her short, white, linen skirt, the bright green cotton top with the short sleeves and the white slip-on sandals that matched her bag. Today she had scraped her hair back and secured it with a band to keep it off her neck. She looked cool and fresh, even though she didn't feel it. Like him, she had not slept well. From his tone, she did not doubt that she was the cause of his lack of sleep, and she was not sure whether she was flattered or annoyed that her shift in identity had somehow involved him.

The vibes she was getting from him as they drank coffee, standing side by side, was that there was a withholding in him rather than a withdrawal as such. He was assessing her, trying to fathom her, reserving his judgment perhaps, as well as calling a halt to whatever sexual attraction he had felt for her.

Was he rejecting her, as she had supposed he might? He now knew that she was not ready for a casual affair, with him or anybody else. Either way, there was regret, sadness. She did care what he thought of her.

'Well,' she said, looking at her watch, 'time to open the doors.' Grant raised his eyebrows at her, saying nothing, as she swallowed the last of her coffee and turned to hurry away from him. They had not bothered to sit down and get too comfortable.

Sister Albertina was there before her, in the act of drawing back the heavy bolts on the thick wooden door. 'Oh, good morning, Dr Lane. Looks like another sweltering day. That means plenty of foot-care for us, eh? Lots of corns, blisters, plantar warts, athlete's foot.'

'Yes.'

'All that stuff is better than some of the trenchfoot we get in the winter. You know, all those homeless guys trudging about with wet socks and boots for hours on end,' the nun said with a shudder. 'Never thought I'd see a case in this city, but I've seen more than I care to comment on.'

The stout woman, who was dressed in a royal blue habit today, with a knee-length skirt and the traditional triangular head gear falling down to shoulder level, looked her usual cheerful self nonetheless. She smiled at Titia, showing her large, square teeth set in a benign, yet no-nonsense face that was shiny with cleanliness and heat. 'How are you today?' she added, perhaps detecting, from long experience, a touch of something subdued in her colleague.

'Fine, thank you,' Titia said. 'Glad to be here, for a change of pace. There's something nice about working in a church. It certainly makes a change from a hospital atmosphere.'

'Yes, it does,' the nun agreed, preparing to swing open the door. 'It reminds us that this is where the work of

God *ought* to be done, the type of work we are doing. There's a quote in the Bible, in the Book of Job… ''I was eyes to the blind, and feet was I to the lame.'' I always think of that when I'm here. Maybe I'll have that as my epitaph!' She grinned at Titia.

Smiling back, Titia knew that the other woman had a wisdom that she herself only aspired to so far, in spite of the common assertion by some people that nuns led narrow lives in which they could not understand the angst of those who married, had children and generally lived away from the security of a sisterhood.

Several young people of about fifteen or sixteen, whom Titia had never seen before, came in through the doorway first. 'Can we get something to eat here?' one of the girls asked. She looked very young and vulnerable, with a clear complexion and baby-fine hair, cut short. In each ear she had several metal studs. There was a boy with her of about the same age.

'Yes.' Titia pointed down the passage. 'Go down there to the Eating Place. Help yourself to whatever you want.'

'Is it free?' the girl asked tentatively, as others in the crowd jostled past her to get in.

'Yes, it's all free,' Titia said kindly, feeling a sobering sense of *déjà vu* as she looked into the girl's anxious face, a face in which bravado, or *cool*, as it was still called from the time of her own youth, was overshadowed by the basic needs of the moment.

'Can we see a doctor after?' the boy chipped in. He was thin and pale, appearing to be malnourished.

'You can,' Titia said. 'I'm Dr Lane. You can see me through there.' She pointed. 'Or, if you want to see a man, there's Dr Saxby there, too. Just sit down in the waiting area and the nurse, Esther, will sort you out. What's your name?'

'I'm Seb, and that is Lu.' He indicated the girl at his side.

'OK,' Titia said. 'We'll see you later. You go and get yourself a decent meal.'

Grant was walking along the passage towards her, greeting some of his patients as he came, so she nodded to the young couple and left for her office area. The sooner she got to work, the better, so that she could put down her own angst, and Grant, out of the forefront of her mind for a while.

Her first patient was Renfrew Brixton, the Jamaican man who had epilepsy. Gratified that he had come back, as she had instructed him to do the previous week, she greeted him warmly as he sat down in her makeshift office.

'How have you been on the new medication?' she asked the colourful man, who was sparsely dressed today in brilliant red satin running shorts and a yellow sleeveless vest over his lean, muscled torso.

'Well, I'm all right so far,' he said, flicking back a long strand of curled hair that had escaped from the tall knitted hat he wore. 'I think it's working all right for me, but I'm feeling a bit low because I haven't got anywhere to live yet, except a doss here and there with friends. They're not much better off than I am.'

'We're keeping an eye out for you here,' Titia said. 'We've got you on our accommodation list for a bedsitter, so if you check here every day with the nurse, Esther, we'll be able to let you know right away if something comes up. Something will come up before the cold weather sets in.'

'I ain't too hopeful,' he said.

'We'll get you something,' she said emphatically. 'You can always sleep here in the church.'

'Thanks. But I'm so tired of everything being tempo-
rary,' he said, with a weary air. 'I'm stuck here, really—
no money to go back where I came from. Don't want to
go, anyway. I've had a few jobs here, day jobs.'

'I've got you an appointment with an immigration lawyer,' Titia said, consulting her notebook. 'His office is
just over the road. It's for later in the day, and here's the
address and phone number.' She wrote the particulars of
the lawyer on a piece of paper. 'He'll tell you how to go
about applying for landed immigrant status.'

'Thanks,' he said.

'Now, I want to take your blood pressure, listen to your
heart, just for the record. And I want to see you on
Wednesday, just to keep an eye on how this new medication is going. Come in any time before then if you're
worried about anything.'

'Right,' he said.

When Mr Brixton had gone, Sister Albertina came in.
'Dr Lane,' she said, 'would you take a look at Dodge's
feet, please? I've just bathed them, as usual, but he's got
a few cuts which are obviously infected. I don't like the
look of them. You know, with all the bacteria around
these days that are resistant to the common antibiotics, I
get uneasy when I see skin abrasions that don't heal well,
that get infected. He's in the office.'

'How did he get cuts on his feet?' Titia asked. 'Has
he had his shoes stolen again?'

'You guessed it,' Sister Albertina said with cheerful
resignation. 'The usual story. He took off his shoes while
he was sleeping on a park bench on Saturday. When he
woke up they were gone. In this sort of heat, plus the
dirt, feet get infected so quickly. I've got him another
pair of shoes and some nice new socks that we had donated.'

'Lead on,' Titia said, smiling.

'Hi, Tishy. Nice to see you,' Dodge said, smiling at her from where he sat in the office, his newly washed feet propped up on a foot stool that was draped with a towel. 'I've been careless again with my shoes. They weren't much good anyway.'

Against the white of the towel the cuts and abrasions on his swollen feet stood out sharply, each cut surrounded by a red area.

'How did your feet get into this shape?' Titia said.

'He missed a few days of coming here,' Sister Albertina said meaningfully.

'So you've been partying,' Titia said, putting it politely, 'and you neglected to come to get your feet attended to.'

'That's about it,' Dodge said, only slightly cowed. 'I know I shouldn't have.'

'In this hot, humid weather,' she said, 'a small cut can become infected very quickly, especially when you're not wearing socks.'

She took a culture swab out of a cupboard in the office. With the cotton-tipped stick she took a specimen of the exudate in the cuts, then put it in the culture medium in the test tube that went with it.

Carefully she explained to Dodge what she was doing. Sometimes the people who came into the clinic were suspicious of some of the procedures, so Titia knew that one had to go carefully. Some of them had reason to be suspicious, as they had not always encountered good care or sympathetic attitudes in the past. No one wanted to have something done to them if they did not fully understand what was being done.

'We'll send these to the hospital lab for culture and sensitivity tests,' she said to Sister Albertina and Dodge.

'I don't like the look of these feet. In the meantime, we'll give him an IV drip with some broad-spectrum antibiotics. Take him into the men's examination room and we'll get him to lie down there.'

'Right,' Sister Albertina said. 'What about the feet themselves? What shall I put on them?'

'Clean the cuts with Betadine, then put on a non-stick gauze dressing and a cotton cling bandage. He needs cotton socks over the lot to keep dirt and dust off the dressing.'

As Dodge hobbled out of the office, supported by Sister Albertina, Titia gathered up a plastic bag of intravenous fluid and an IV giving set. Addressing Dodge's retreating back, she admonished him, 'Make sure you come back tomorrow, Dodge, without fail. I'll be in there in a moment to put up an IV—with your consent, of course.'

'Anything you say, Doc,' he called back, chastened.

Sighing, Titia unlocked the cupboard where they kept their antibiotics and the vials of sterile water for mixing up powdered drugs.

When Dodge was ensconced in the men's examination room, with fluid and antibiotics dripping slowly into a vein in his arm and Sister Albertina putting the finishing touches to the dressings on his feet, Titia went to the sink to wash her hands.

'I'm going to get myself a cup of coffee, Sister Albertina,' she said, suddenly feeling in need of more caffeine. 'Back in a few minutes.'

Grant was behind some curtains of one of the examination bays. She could hear the low murmur of his voice, questioning a patient.

'Have one of the chocolate chip muffins,' Ted invited her from behind the counter in the Eating Place. 'They've just come in, fresh out of the oven. I guarantee it.'

In her sensitive emotional state, Titia felt a familiar constriction in her throat at Ted's mundane words, a sharp pang of remembrance. Grant had brought her such an offering, with the hot chocolate, when he had comforted her in this church in her time of dire need. 'Thanks, Ted, I will have one,' she said.

With a flourish, Ted placed a large muffin on a plate for her. 'There you go,' he said. 'Oh, hi, there, Dr Saxby. Same for you?'

Titia swung round, holding her cup and plate, to see Grant closing the gap between the door and the counter.

'I'll say yes to whatever that is...please,' Grant said.

Remembering how they had kissed yesterday, Titia felt her face reddening as she made her way to a table in a far corner of the large room. If they were to have words, she wanted some privacy.

'I'm only taking a short break,' she said when he joined her, aware that she must have sounded defensive.

'Sure,' he said, sitting down opposite her, his eyes going over her flushed face. 'I'm only taking a short break myself so you don't have to worry that I'm going to foist myself on you.'

'Oh, I'm not worried,' she said brightly. 'It's all in a day's work.'

'Being brittle doesn't suit you, Titia,' he said quietly, fixing her with a considering stare.

'I'm not sure you know what suits me, Grant,' she said. 'Let's just concentrate on our work, shall we?'

Then, sipping coffee, she felt annoyance and a contrary disappointment, even though the retreat into work was a relief.

'Tell me the latest with Rita, please,' she said quickly. 'When do you think she can be discharged? I thought I would go over to Cedar Glen during my lunch-break to take a final look at the apartment, make sure it's aired out. I've got a few good leads with regard to furniture so I may go over there tomorrow after work with some stuff people have promised me.'

'That's great,' he said. 'Maybe I'll discharge her at the end of this week. Don't want to rush it. I'm making quite sure that her insulin dose is sorted out in relation to her blood sugar.'

'The longer she stays in, the better.'

'As for the guy with the malaria, he's pretty good,' Grant said, between mouthfuls of coffee. 'That could have had an entirely different outcome if he hadn't come in when he did.'

'Excuse me, it's back to work for me.' Titia stood up, needing to get away. She left the Eating Place quickly, finding that she could scarcely face Grant now that her attraction to him was out in the open. If only they had not allowed things to go so far so quickly yesterday. Now she was acutely aware of every physical nuance between them. If he hadn't touched her, if he hadn't brushed his lips against hers exactly a week ago, she would have been all right.

Esther, the nurse, motioned her into the office when she got back to the clinic. 'Dr Lane, can I have a quick word?'

'Sure.'

'About that young couple who came in this morning,' Esther said, closing the door behind them. 'I've put her in your office and the young man in Dr Saxby's office, although they wanted to stay together and you will want to confer with Dr Saxby when he's seen the boy. I think there's something serious going on there.'

'Seb and Lu?' Titia queried. 'Those kids who look about fifteen?'

'That's right,' Esther confirmed. 'They're seventeen, actually. They're both malnourished, and he looks pretty sick as well. I wouldn't be surprised if he's got AIDS. They both seem scared, as though they have a pretty good idea there's something wrong. I got a preliminary history—they are both runaways, been on the streets, in the hostel scene, for about a year.'

A sharp sense of sadness rendered Titia momentarily speechless. 'There but for the grace of God go I.' The old familiar adage came to her mind. Emotionally labile as she was from her confrontation with Grant the previous day, she felt that she would like to go away somewhere quiet by herself and have a good cry. Sometimes you thought you had successfully buried emotions, then out of the blue they popped to the surface.

'It's the usual home scene,' Esther said, filling the breach. 'I don't have to go into the details with you, I know, Dr Lane. I've put some of it in the preliminary notes so that you don't have to go through it all again with them. They've been getting by with odd jobs. They both need a safe haven.'

'Drugs?' Titia found her voice at last.

'They say not,' Esther said. 'I believe them. But who knows what happened in the beginning? Anyway, I think they both need a good medical work-up.'

Grant came into the office, and Esther repeated what she had said to Titia.

The girl, Lu, was sitting beside Titia's desk, hunched forward, her hands clasped tightly in her lap. She wore thin shorts and a sleeveless top, with the usual knapsack on the floor beside her. Her face was pale, thin and drawn, the eyes shadowed beyond her years.

'Hello,' Titia said, as she sat down at her desk and reached for the preliminary notes which Esther had left

in a folder. Quickly she scanned them. The girl did not
feel well, she had little energy. With any other girl Titia
might have suspected anorexia nervosa for the girl was
abnormally thin, but, given that she was living in strait-
ened circumstances, her thinness was most likely not due
to a voluntary lack of food.

'Have you anything to add to what you told the nurse?'
she asked kindly.

'Well, I…I did have a miscarriage just after I came to
live in the hostels… I lost a lot of blood,' the girl said
hesitantly. 'I haven't felt really right since that time.'
When she saw Titia's questioning look, the girl added,
'It's something I don't like talking about. That's why I
didn't tell the nurse.'

'I understand,' Titia said gently.

'It was my stepfather—he was responsible. That's why
I left home.'

'I see,' Titia said, keeping her tone neutral while anger
boiled within her. 'Did you go to a hospital when you
had that miscarriage?'

'Yeah…Gresham General. I still bleed a lot—that's
one of the reasons I don't feel right.'

'I'll see if I can get hold of your chart from there so
that we can read about it. Now, what I want to do is a
very thorough physical examination—weigh you, test
your urine, then take some blood for tests. I want to see
if you're anemic, for a start,' Titia said, plotting her strat-
egy.

'Oh, I expect I'm that all right,' the girl said.

'I want to do a tuberculin skin test to see if you possibly have tuberculosis because you're so thin. The nurse
has put down here that you have a persistent cough.'

'That's right.'

'Maybe you have some vitamin and mineral deficiencies as well, so perhaps I should start you on folic acid and iron, in tablet form, plus a multivitamin pill. Also, I'd like to do an AIDS test—I have to have your permission for that, of course. The blood for that would be sent to a special lab, and the other tests would be done at University Hospital, after I've taken the blood here.'

'Right,' the girl said, fixing Titia with her pale, tired stare. 'I give permission for everything. There's no point not to, is there?' She gave a wry laugh.

Titia smiled in return. 'I'd like to take you to University Hospital, maybe this afternoon if I can arrange it, for a chest X-ray,' she said. 'And there's a gynaecology resident-in-training there, Dr Lily Wong, whom I'd like you to see if I can arrange that. She's very nice, easy to talk to. If your heavy periods are making you anaemic, we should do something about that.'

'OK.'

Before doing the physical examination, Titia made a few phone calls to the hospital to set up some quick appointments. Doctors at the hospital co-operated with doctors and nurses at the clinic as far as they could, fitting the Open Door patients in their busy schedules. At the clinic they knew which doctors would be sympathetic, and vice versa. Also, Medical Records at Gresham General agreed to send over photocopies of Lu's medical records, in a sealed envelope, by taxi.

With Lu waiting on the examination table, Titia went in to see Grant. 'Hi,' she said, finding him about to examine Seb. 'Could I have a brief word?'

'Sure,' he said, coming out from behind the screening curtains.

'I've arranged to send the girl to the hospital to see a few people and have a chest X-ray,' she explained, as they moved out of earshot. 'Maybe the two of them could go together. We could put them in a taxi, and maybe Sister Albertina could go with them, make sure they get to the right departments.'

'Make sure they go to them, you mean,' he said quietly, moving with her into his office.

'That, too,' she said. 'I think the girl will, definitely.'

'Good idea,' he said thoughtfully. 'We should get them to sleep here for the next few nights, at least until we can see the results of tuberculin skin tests.' They both knew, only too well, that tuberculoses was making a comeback, particularly among street people and AIDS patients and was sometimes resistant to previously effective antibiotics.

'Yes, I agree,' she said.

'I'll get Esther to fix it up for them to stay here,' he said. 'Before you go, there's something I want you to look at on this young man—tell me what you think it is. He's got some sort of skin rash.'

Titia followed Grant back behind the curtains of the examination cubicle where Seb was lying on the table, covered by a thin cotton sheet. Grant pulled the sheet back from the young man's legs. 'Take a look at that, Titia,' Grant said quietly, indicating the small red marks that dotted the young man's thighs.

There was evidence that the areas had been scratched; each small red area had a scab on top of it.

'How long have you had this rash?' Titia asked thoughtfully, running her fingers gently over the skin.

'I had it throughout the winter,' the boy said matter-of-factly. 'It's a bit better now than it was.'

'Have you ever been treated for it?'

'Well, a doctor I went to at the hospital gave me some cortisone cream last winter,' Seb explained, his pale, tired face deadpan. 'I put it on every day, but it didn't do much so I didn't bother to get any more.'

'He's got some on his arms, round his neck and waist, too,' Grant said.

'Could I see?' Titia looked carefully at the small pink marks with the scabs on top. Sometimes AIDS produced a rash in the early stages, but she did not think that was exactly like the rash she was looking at. She was about to tell Grant that she could not say what type of skin disease Seb might have when something about the distribution of the rash, as well as the appearance of the scabs, rang a bell with her, a memory of a coloured picture in her medical book of skin diseases. 'Does it itch a lot?' she added.

'Yeah…drives me crazy at times.'

'Could this be scabies?' Titia said to Grant.

'That's what I was thinking,' he said.

'What's that?' Seb asked, looking at them enquiringly.

'Well, it's caused by a parasite, a mite,' Grant explained. 'It's called the itch mite, or its scientific name is *Sarcoptes scabiei*.'

'Hell.' Seb raised his head off the pillow. 'Have I got that?'

'Could be,' Grant said. 'We'll have to take some skin scrapings to make a firm diagnosis, see if we can find the mite. We need a microscope to see it. We'll start you on some cream, anyway, when we've done that. We won't wait for the result. Do you agree, Dr Lane?'

'Absolutely,' she said. What Grant did not say was that they could not always count on their patients coming back for treatment, so it was necessary to strike while the iron was hot, so to speak. Scabies generally came from circumstances of extreme poverty and lack of cleanliness.

'I suggest that you have a bath while you're here,'

Grant said to their patient, 'then we'll get the nurse to put the first lot of cream on your skin.' To Titia he added, 'Five per cent permethrin cream is best.'

'I see,' she said quietly. 'I've never seen a case of scabies before.'

'Better take a good look,' Grant said.

Titia went back to her own patient, marvelling at how well she and Grant got along together when they were working, how they both loved the work they were doing so that they could put aside any personal considerations. She sighed. It would be lovely if some of that professional calmness could spill over into their personal relationship to smooth out the prickliness that existed between them the moment there was no work to distract them.

It was late by the time Titia finally got to the Eating Place to grab a sandwich for a belated lunch. With the sandwich in a paper bag, she went out to the street to hail a taxi that would take her to Cedar Glen. She was determined that she would go to check on the apartment for Rita to make sure that the paint fumes were dissipating. In her bag she carried a tin of anti-cockroach powder which she intended to sprinkle in the cupboard under the sink and along the skirting-boards of the kitchen.

As the taxi took her the short distance to the apartment complex, she hastily chomped on the sandwich. There had been a lot to do that morning to take her mind off herself and her relationship with Grant.

The apartment door was open when she got there, through which she could see several large fans blowing air from the rooms out the open windows.

'Oh, hi! Dr Lane, isn't it?' Connie, the janitor, emerged

from the kitchen. She was now clothed in shorts and a T-shirt against the heat.

'Yes.' Titia smiled at her. 'I've just come to see if there's anything else we should be doing here before we move in furniture.'

'Well, I'm airing the place out, as you can see. It won't normally be as hot as this. I've an air-conditioner in the bedroom window, and when you get some curtains up they'll keep some of the heat out.'

Relieved to see that everything was under control, Titia set about leaving careful lines of anti-cockroach powder in strategic positions, smiling to herself as she remembered how she and Grant had laughed when they had trapped the cockroach in the jar. Connie watched her.

'I reckon that woman is going to be real grateful for the way you've organized this place for her,' Connie said.

'Let's hope we manage to get rid of the cockroaches first.' Titia smiled. 'Then I think she'll love it.'

'I left all the kitchen cupboards open, as you can see. There hasn't been a cockroach in sight today, I can vouch for that. They hate fresh air and light, and they hate chlorine. I can tell by the smell that you put lots of chlorine about the other day.'

'We sure did.'

'I'll shut the windows later and get the air-conditioner going,' Connie said. 'When do you think she'll be moving in?'

'Next weekend, maybe. I've got curtains and we're rounding up some furniture. We'll make sure you've got two months' rent in advance. That's going to come from the authorities.' Even as she said the words, Titia knew that she would have her work cut out for her to get the place fixed up in time. There were several people she had asked for furniture. It was now a question of getting the stuff transported. 'Someone's going to lend us a van.'

By the time four-thirty came, Titia could look back on an absolutely hectic day. There had been a lot of behind-the-scenes arranging to do for their patients. Sister Albertina had escorted the two young people to the hospital, and kept an eagle eye on them while they visited the departments where appointments had been made for them, then had brought them back to the Open Door for a meal. Esther, in the meantime, had made sure that they had beds to sleep in for a few days, clean clothes and the anti-scabies treatment organized.

Titia had performed the tuberculin skin tests, superficial injections into the skin, which would yield results after two or three days. If positive, indicating that the patient had antibodies to TB, this would be indicated by a red, raised area of the skin around the injection site. A positive result could indicate that a person had the active disease, or it could mean that they had at some time encountered the disease and produced antibodies to it.

As she was preparing to leave, Grant came into her office.

'Goodnight, Titia,' he said. 'No doubt we'll meet at the hospital during the week.'

'Yes, I expect so,' she said.

It was on the Thursday of that week that Grant sought her out in the emergency department of the hospital.

'Hi, Titia,' he said, coming into the office where she stood punching data into the computer, putting his hand briefly on her shoulder to get her attention. 'I thought you'd like to know that I called Esther at the clinic about that young couple, Seb and Lu. She said that both the tuberculin tests are strongly positive.'

'I thought they might be when I looked at them yesterday,' she said.

'Well, they're more so now…particularly for Seb,' Grant said. 'Also, I went to Radiology to take a look at the chest X-rays. He's got a shadow on one of his lungs, right lower lobe, indicative of tuberculosis.'

'Oh, heck,' Titia said, sighing. 'That's not great for someone on the street. I guess we should start him on the anti-tuberculosis drugs right away.'

'Yes. I told Esther that I'd drive over there this afternoon and write up the drug orders so that she can make a start, and get Seb and Lu to stay at the clinic,' he said. 'We'll need to find them a permanent place to live.'

'I guess we still have to wait a while for the results of the AIDS tests,' she said, looking up at him. His touch had made her more acutely aware that she was missing him.

'Yes…' His regard was intense and she found she could not look away. 'Have you got a few minutes, Titia? I want to know where I stand with you. It's burning me up. And don't pretend you don't know what I mean.'

Titia looked around hastily. There was no one else in sight.

'I hope you don't think of me as one of those self-serving do-gooders,' he added tersely.

'No. You like to get your hands too dirty, in every sense, to be one of those,' she said truthfully. 'And you're much too good at your job.'

'I'm relieved,' he said, a hint of sarcasm in his tone. 'So…where do I stand with you?'

'I'm not ready for an affair…with you or anybody else,' she said quickly, feeling her face tinge with colour.

Any minute now someone else might come into the office. Also, that wasn't strictly true. The more time they spent with each other, the more difficult it was for her not to agree to anything on his terms. Yet she sensed that when such an affair was over, she would be devastated. 'I…think we should confine ourselves largely to work and…see how it goes.' That was an admission of sorts, and she saw his eyes darken in response. 'It's not my style to jump into something with my eyes closed—especially not with you.'

'What does that mean?'

'We…we obviously do have some emotional baggage between us, left over from the past,' she said.

'I don't want to frighten you away, Titia. That's the last thing I want,' he said. 'No assumptions, no strings… for now. Hmm?'

'You want to add me to your list?' she said.

He shrugged. 'If I had you, I wouldn't have anybody else.'

'You said there was safety in numbers,' she reminded him.

He had the grace to smile. 'I could forgo that.'

'Until you got fed up with me,' she said tersely. 'I'd like to have the opportunity to get to know you, Grant, I admit that,' she said. 'Really know you as a person— not just as Dr Grant Saxby.'

A nurse was hurrying along the corridor towards the office, signalling the end of the conversation which seemed to Titia to be bordering on the bizarre. The tension between her and Grant seemed to crackle in the air, so she felt that the nurse would surely feel it too.

Grant placed a hand over hers on the desk. 'You may well get fed up first. No strings?' he said urgently, his face taut.

'All right, no strings,' she agreed. Privately she vowed to throw herself more deeply into her work.

Grant left the office before the nurse came in. As Titia watched his tall, commanding figure striding away from her down the corridor, his lab coat billowing around him, her heart was beating fast.

CHAPTER EIGHT

OVER the next three to four weeks the summer heat continued, then fairly suddenly gave way to cooler autumn weather halfway through the fourth week. There was a violent thunderstorm, then the change. Titia gave a sigh of relief when she went to the Open Door clinic on the Wednesday of that week, walking in rain from the streetcar stop to the side door of St Barnabas's church where the staff entered. Much as she loved summer and, like everybody else, complained about the rigours of winter, the humidity of August in Gresham got you down by the end of the month.

'Morning, Dr Lane,' Esther greeted her as she entered the office in the clinic. 'We're both early today. Must be something to do with the cooler weather, eh? That was some storm in the night!'

'It was,' Titia agreed, smiling a welcome at the nurse. 'Maybe the rain will scare off some of our regulars. What do you think?'

'Well, it will have cleared all the people out from the park, that's for sure. They will have gone to one of the hostels, I guess.'

'That's great,' Titia said. 'I could use a slack day. I want to go through some of the outstanding paperwork. I'm going to get a coffee. Want one, Esther?'

'I've just had one, thanks.'

Titia made her way to the Eating Place, wanting to get a quick breakfast before the onslaught of patients and hungry people.

'Morning, Dr Lane,' Ted greeted her from behind his counter. 'We've got some great muffins today—peach, banana, cranberry, bran, blueberry, as well as the inevitable chocolate chip. Take your pick.'

'Wow!' Titia poured herself coffee. 'That's a difficult choice. I'll have a cranberry, please, Ted.'

'Good choice,' Ted remarked, placing an oversized muffin on a plate for her.

Seated at a corner table, where she sometimes sat with Grant, she sipped her coffee and ate the delicious, warm muffin. Thinking of Grant, she realized that on the days he was not at the clinic she missed him with a sharp poignancy, was actually missing him more and more each day when she was the only doctor there. Staring absently into space, she thought back over the past three to four weeks, acknowledging that her emotional equilibrium was becoming more and more unreliable.

She had deliberately avoided being alone with Grant, both at the clinic and at the hospital whenever they had reason to confer about a patient. It was not difficult as both places were crowded with staff and patients. All his efforts to be alone with her had been foiled by her.

Now that very success was taking its toll on her as she was coming to admit that she liked being with him, very much. Obviously he knew what she was up to as his eyes would gleam with a wry amusement as she manoeuvred to avoid him. Sometimes he would raise his eyebrows at her; at other times he would wink at her when she had orchestrated a particularly clever avoidance technique or executed a feat of studied indifference. He was definitely biding his time, while she was trying to hold on to her resolution to get through her residency training, before getting involved with him or any other man.

Sighing, she knew that her resolution was faltering.

There was also the irritating, contrary fear that he would lose interest in her. Quite frequently he flirted outrageously with the lovely Maralyn, who reciprocated in full measure by pouting her shapely lips, batting her long eyelashes at him and swinging her hips when she walked to and fro in his presence. He rewarded her by staring appreciatively. At those times Titia pursed her lips and looked away. The truth was, she didn't know what to do, didn't know how to respond to him. She had got into the habit of denying herself.

Back in the front hall she saw Sister Albertina unlocking the big main door. 'Good morning, Dr Lane. Now, this is my sort of weather.' She beamed good-naturedly. 'I love the rain. I feel my energy returning.'

'Yes, I love fall, too…all those lovely red leaves.'

'Ah…'

In her makeshift office, Titia unlocked a drawer and got out some lab reports she had to look at more closely and then file.

Over the past few weeks she and Grant had found a room for their patient Renfrew Brixton, the epileptic, and they had found a small two-roomed flat above a shop on the same street as St Barnabas's for the young couple, Seb and Lu. They loved the flat and had been helped to redecorate it and find furniture. Almost every day they came to the Eating Place for meals, then to the clinic for the tuberculosis treatment. One good thing, they had not tested positive for AIDS. Things were very gradually getting sorted out for them.

Half an hour later Titia checked the waiting area. 'Who's first?' she called out.

Contrary to expectation, the morning was so busy that she ate a quick salad lunch at her desk and then went right on working. The waiting area never emptied itself.

The rain had initially kept people away, but then they came in droves to get out of the wet and, once in, remembered health problems they had not attended to. Titia found herself looking at infected teeth and gums, skin diseases, allergies of all types, the usual chronic coughs, as well as patients with more serious complaints such as chest pain, retention of urine, abnormal uterine bleeding, and so on. At four-thirty she glanced wearily at the clock.

Going out to the waiting area, she saw Sister Albertina shepherding the last patient out to the office. 'Foot care!' Sister Albertina said to her. 'Looks like the end of the day for us…and if it isn't, the evening nurses can see to it.'

They exchanged commiserating smiles. 'Goodnight, then. See you next week,' Titia said. Firmly she shut the door of the women's examination room and sat down at her desk. It was great to have a little quiet time.

That day she had ordered so many laboratory tests of various sorts that she now had to file the duplicate request forms in a large file under 'Lab Results Pending.' When the results came back she would have to put them in the appropriate case history files, then institute appropriate treatment. It was not easy to contact patients when they had no fixed address—she just had to hope that they would come back when asked.

Just as she finished she heard a commotion out in the corridor, and hoped that the two nurses who were on the evening and night shift would have arrived and were ready to deal with anything that required medical attention. She got up and collected her light raincoat, umbrella and bag, ready to go home, then she raked a brush through her untidy hair just as there was a knock on the door.

'Come in,' she called. Maybe this day was staying true to form and she was not going to get away that easily.

Esther came in, her tired face looking worried. 'Dr Lane, a young guy just came in, said he was a friend of Renfrew Brixton,' she explained hastily. 'Apparently he, Renfrew, is in a semi-comatose state over the road in his bedsitter. This guy, the friend, says it looks as though he's taken too many pills. The two nurses who just came have gone over there, plus a few of the guys from the Eating Place, with a stretcher to bring him back over here. I'm sure glad you're still here.'

'Oh, hell!' Titia said. 'Not an overdose! Does the friend think it's attempted suicide?'

The nurse shrugged, her face haggard. 'I sure hope it isn't that. The friend seemed to think that it wasn't, but he did hesitate a bit when I asked him that. He had to admit that Renfrew had seemed a bit depressed over the last few days because the immigration thing doesn't seem to be going anywhere very quickly. Apparently he mentioned this morning that he felt like he was about to have a seizure so he took the pills…then maybe he got confused and worried, and then took more.'

'Oh, no,' Titia groaned, anxiety flooding over her, 'surely not! I've been giving him phenobarbital, but I only gave him enough each time to cover him for a few days, just to avoid this sort of thing. Not for a minute did I think he was suicidal.'

They looked at each other in silence for a moment, weighing up the odds.

'Maybe he wasn't. Maybe he's been saving them up,' Esther suggested. 'Or maybe it's purely accidental. You know what patients are like—they have a couple of beers when they know they shouldn't, take pills, then forget they've taken them and take more later. Some of them think that if two or three pills are good for them, maybe five or six would be, then they forget…'

'Oh, Esther,' Titia sighed, 'I do hope you're right. But he's a bright guy.'

'Anyway, I was wondering if we should just call an ambulance right away and get him over to University Hospital,' Esther went on hurriedly, 'or deal with him here initially ourselves, and then call the ambulance. I know darn well he won't want to go to the hospital— although he probably won't be in any condition to make a choice.'

'We don't have a choice really,' Titia said grimly. 'Yes, we'll assess him here, put up an IV, then wash out his stomach if it definitely looks like he's taken something. Let's get the treatment room ready, Esther.'

Together they went quickly to the small treatment room where they dealt with emergencies, before transporting patients to hospital by ambulance. Esther took a sterile wrapped tray out of one of the cupboards. 'This is the stomach lavage tray,' she said. 'Haven't had to use this for a while, that's why I keep it sterile. It has various sizes of orogastric and nasogastric tubes in it, plus the large syringes for the lavage. I assume you'll want to send the stomach washings to the hospital lab, Dr Lane, to see what's in the stomach?'

'Yes. And I'll take blood for the toxicology lab when we get to Emergency to save time,' she said hurriedly. 'If you put up the IV, Esther, dextrose-saline, I'll put down the gastric tube, then you can help me do the wash-out. If he's not unconscious, he's going to put up a bit of resistance to that,' Titia said.

'You bet!' Esther agreed, as she unwrapped the tray and Titia began to sort through the equipment in it.

'You've got the mouth gag there, and the McGill forceps for helping you get the tube in if necessary.'

'I may want to intubate him with an endotracheal tube, in which case I'll need to spray the back of his throat with the anaesthetic spray because he'll sure put up resistance to that if he's not right out,' Titia said. There had been no time for her to don her lab coat, and the nurse was also in her outdoor clothing. Quickly they set out items of vital equipment on a small mobile table.

'We have a flexible bronchoscope here, too,' Esther reminded her, 'if you have trouble getting the endotracheal tube in place. I've only seen that used once here. It's sterile.'

'Great! Let's have that on hand. The first priority, Esther, is to intubate him, give him continuous oxygen, get him on a monitor for his vital signs, then get the IV in pronto. He will already have absorbed a good deal of the drug, I should imagine, so we need to get the IV fluids running in fast to counteract that before we get the stomach tube down and wash out the stomach.'

'Right! I'm going into the office to get the IV stuff,' Esther said. 'I assume it will be ten per cent glucose in saline?'

'Yes,' Titia said, thinking ahead with lightning speed to all they would have to do, in order of priority. 'I'll need some IV potassium chloride as well, and a diuretic to make sure he passes a lot of urine to get the drug out of his system.'

'OK,' Esther said. 'Back in a few minutes. I'll call the ambulance while I'm there.'

'Great! The sooner we get him to Emergency, the better. He may need some IV plasma, which we haven't got here,' Titia said.

When Esther was out of the room, Titia readied her

equipment quickly and methodically, checking that the oxygen cylinder was full—the first priority was to ensure that their patient was breathing properly. Her anxious mind was going over how it could have happened, and whether she had been remiss in her duty. She felt sick with apprehension...and a sudden overwhelming guilt.

Thank God, she thought, that they had the basic equipment at the clinic for resuscitation. They had monitors for the continuous recording of heart rate and blood pressure, which had been donated by the manufacturers, as well as the cylinders of oxygen and the equipment for administering it.

'The ambulance is on its way, with paramedics,' Esther said as she hurried back into the room, carrying the equipment for giving the intravenous fluid and drugs. She proceeded to open up the outer cover of the one-litre bag of fluid and insert the plastic giving line.

'We're all set now, Esther,' Titia said. 'So, intubation first to keep the airway open. I'll need help from you with that initially, with cricoid pressure on the throat, and you can hand me the local anaesthetic spray for the larynx. You know all that, Esther, I know,' she added. 'I'm just thinking aloud.'

There were sounds of raised voices and a renewed commotion out in the main church hall. Titia went to meet her patient.

It was half past eleven in the evening, dark and raining, when Titia left the emergency department of University Hospital to walk through the main doors to the outside. The fresh, cool, moist air played against her heated face in a welcome gust, and she took several deep, calming breaths as she stood under the portico. For a few moments she sat on a low concrete wall to collect her thoughts.

Renfrew Brixton was all right, now in the acute care unit of the hospital. When he had come into the clinic he had been comatose but rousable. She and Esther had intubated him and performed all the other immediate measures to counteract the overdose. Now he was awake but groggy, apologetic and resigned to being in the hospital. The friend who had come in with him had told her that he didn't think Renfrew had taken the drugs deliberately, that it had been an accident, but Titia was not going to rule it out yet. They would take all necessary precautions. She felt completely drained.

A taxi came into view through the rain, which was quite heavy now, and stopped at the entrance to let out two people. On impulse, Titia got up and went over to the car.

'Are you free?' she asked the driver.

'Yep,' he said. 'Where to, ma'am?'

Titia climbed into the back of the cab. Then she gave the driver an address that was not her own.

The rain was lashing down when she got out of the cab and paid the driver outside the big Victorian house in the quiet residential street.

'Night, ma'am,' he said.

She walked up the garden path and rang the doorbell of the second-floor flat. A moment later a masculine voice sounded through the intercom beside the bell. 'Hello?'

'It's me…Titia,' she said, aware that her voice wobbled and that she could not control it.

There were a few seconds of silence. 'Titia!' he said. 'I'm coming down.'

When the door opened onto a dimly lit hall moments

later she said, 'H-hello, Grant. I just wanted to see you.' It registered with her vaguely that he wore a dark blue dressing-gown over pyjamas, and that he looked tousled and very, very dear.

Without a word he reached forward to grasp her arm, draw her into the warmth of the hall and close the door. For moments they stood looking at each other. 'Tishy,' he said softly, 'what is it?'

She noticed that the expression on his face was a mixture of emotions—of concern, puzzlement and a kind of warm pleasure that made her heart begin to beat faster with a reciprocal feeling. It was so good to see him.

'I…'

'Hell, you're soaking wet, and you're shivering.' He looked her up and down slowly, taking in the wet skirt and top. 'You're carrying your coat. Why didn't you put it on?'

'I…I didn't think,' she said, looking down vaguely at the coat, bag and umbrella she was carrying, as though they didn't belong to her.

'Sweetheart, what is it?' he said, his voice deep with concern. 'Are you in some sort of trouble?'

'No…I don't think so,' she said absently. 'Something has happened, but I think it's all right now. I had to come.'

Decisively, he took the things she was holding and put an arm round her shoulders. 'Come on,' he said, leading her to the staircase. Obediently she allowed herself to be led, until they were in the sanctuary of his flat. To her it felt like home because that was where he was. Looking at her with concern, he put his arms around her and pulled her against the warmth of his strong body, kissing her deeply, warmly, as though to snap her out of the somnambulistic state she seemed to be in.

'Sweetheart…tell me,' he coerced her. 'Are you all right?'

'Yes,' she said, standing in the circle of his arms. 'I think I'm more all right, really, than I've been in a long time, although I don't feel exactly great.' She felt very sober, very certain.

Grant kissed her again, holding her strongly as though he never intended to release her.

'Something has happened, though, hasn't it? And you're still shaking.'

He swung her up in his arms and carried her to his bedroom, where he deposited her on top of a down duvet on the double bed. Then he folded the other half of the duvet over her, covering her up to her chin. He lay down beside her on his stomach, from which position he gently stroked the wet hair from her forehead, his face alight with a strange expression of tenderness.

Kissing her on her cheeks, mouth and eyelids, he said, 'Tell me.'

'Renfrew Brixton took an overdose of drugs,' she said flatly. 'I don't know whether he intended to. I've just spent the last few hours resuscitating him, then staying with him in the hospital. He seems all right now…but I'm not sure I am. I prescribed his drugs, I feel responsible. And I…I feel that I failed him, Grant.'

Grant kissed her softly and looked deep into her eyes, before saying, 'Welcome to the club.'

Bells rang in her memory—he had told her that he had felt like a failure with her when she had upped and left his sister's apartment all those years ago, just leaving a brief, inadequate note. Understanding came to her like a sharp pang to the heart. Soberly she returned his intent regard, as though she were looking keep into his soul. Still she shivered under the warmth of the duvet.

'You'd better get out of those wet clothes,' he said. 'I'll find you something to put on.'

While she quickly undressed and piled her wet clothes on the floor on the far side of the bed, Grant searched in a drawer for a spare pair of pyjamas. Under the cover of the duvet, she got into them while he watched her, smiling.

'I've always wanted to get you into that position,' he quipped, his eyes dark. 'I'm going to get you a glass of brandy. Then you'd better tell me more.'

With Grant reclining on the bed beside her, she sipped the brandy and talked until she had no more to add.

'Look, Tishy, I have always found it best not to assume that it's an attempted suicide until you've had a chance to talk to the patient and get all the facts when he's wide awake,' he said thoughtfully. 'When we know the facts, of course, we can't ignore them if it turns out to be the other way. Until then, don't come down too heavily on the side of suicide. I think he has too much of a phlegmatic personality for that—and I'm not just saying that to cheer you up. I'll go to see him with you tomorrow, if you like.'

Titia nodded and put the empty glass on the bedside table. 'Thank you,' she said. 'I'd like that very much.'

Grant rolled over so that he could place his elbows on either side of her body, with his face a few inches above hers. 'Why did you come to me?' he said.

'I wanted to be with you,' she whispered.

When he pulled aside the duvet and got in beside her she opened her arms to him, burying her face in the warmth of his shoulder.

'Darling…my darling,' he murmured against her mouth, moving a hand over her breasts under the thin cotton of the voluminous pyjama jacket. 'My God…

Titia, you're so lovely. I'm very glad you came. You realize, don't you, that I'm not going to let you get out of this bed?' When his mouth found hers, kissing her hungrily, she responded with all the exploding, pent-up frustration of the past weeks. She arched her body against his, holding him as he was holding her.

Sharply he pulled back from her, his eyes blazing down into hers. 'What does this mean to you? I have to know…because I'm going to make love to you.' The urgency and sureness in his voice brooked no denial. 'Why me, Titia? You must have other people you can talk to.'

'Because I love you…I love you so much. I can't go on any longer.' She looked into his face, unflinching. 'If that offer to live with you is still open, I want to take it,' she whispered. 'On your terms. I don't care.'

'Oh, God…' His hands were on her then, stroking her skin, unbuttoning the jacket.

Awkwardly Titia shrugged out of the jacket, welcoming his touch which felt like fire on her sensitized skin. 'Oh, Grant,' she murmured as he undressed beside her. Then she felt his hands caressing her.

'Tishy…is this what you want? I have to be sure.' Grant's breath caressed her ear as he murmured the words urgently.

'Yes…yes, please.'

Titia woke as the grey light of dawn came through a crack in the curtains of Grant's bedroom, just as it had woken her in Loretta's room at the medical residence eight years ago. Now she woke at dawn because she was a doctor and had to go to work, not because she was a runaway.

Carefully she turned her head on the pillow so that she

could look at Grant's dark head beside her own. Instead of waking up to loneliness, she now awoke to a poignant sense of joy and wonder that she should actually be there with him. Now she was a mature woman, with the means of earning her own living, not dependent on anyone, and she was the maker of her own destiny.

Throughout the night they had made love, then slept. A sense of rightness had pervaded their coming together. Now she revelled in the warmth of his body against her own, his arm flung across her protectively and possessively. How strange were the ways of fate—they seemed to have met again by accident when she had assumed that they would most likely never see each other again, and now here they were, never to be parted again if she could help it. How close she had come to not finding him.

Grant's eyes opened and looked into hers, as though she had willed him to wake. 'Hey.' He smiled lazily. 'I guess you're waiting for me to drive you to work. Hmm?' With that, he gathered her into his arms.

'Sure.' She smiled back. 'I expect my clothes are still wet. Just as well I carry a clean scrub suit with me at all times, isn't it?'

'Mmm.' He nuzzled her neck. 'So you want to stay with me, do you? On my terms?'

'Yes.' She smiled. 'No reservations whatsoever...if you still want me.'

'Why?' he murmured.

'I adore you,' she said. 'I couldn't live without you because it wouldn't be living.'

'Dr Laetitia Lane,' he said, 'I will take you in any way, shape or form...any way you want to present yourself, red hair and all. And with any name you care to take.'

'Oh, Grant.' She laughed with abject relief and love, returning his hug.

'I feel as though I've always loved you,' he said softly, squashing her fears that he wanted her physically but did not love her in the same way, 'as though you were part of me, flesh and blood. There's no way I could ever deny you. I'd given up on hoping that I would see you again.'

Tears filled her eyes. 'I know,' she whispered, realizing with amazement that it was true, almost as though all this had been pre-ordained.

'So you'll take me on any terms?' he murmured.

'Yes…please.'

'Will you marry me, then, Dr Laetitia Lane, as soon as it can be arranged?' he smiled down at her. 'Please.'

In answer she kissed him. 'Nothing could stop me,' she added, her happiness shining in her eyes. 'I've come home, Grant.'

'This time it's going to be permanent,' he said. 'That means for ever.'

As the rain pattered against the window they lay secure in each other's arms. To Titia this was the first day of her future, a future in which she could truly let the past go and look ahead with the man she loved.

MILLS & BOON®

Makes any time special

Copyright © Harlequin Enterprises Limited 1997
All rights reserved

Enjoy a romantic novel from
Mills & Boon®

Presents...™   *Enchanted™*   TEMPTATION®

Historical Romance™   ✚ MEDICAL ROMANCE™

MAT1

MILLS & BOON®

MEDICAL ROMANCE™

WINNING HER BACK by Lilian Darcy
Medicine and marriage, Southshore has it all

Dr Grace Gaines was devastated by the loss of her baby,
more so as it became clear that her husband Marcus had not
wanted the child. Their marriage under threat, Marcus had
taken a six month break, and now he was back. Would they
stay married or not…

RULES OF ENGAGEMENT by Jean Evans

After her Uncle Jon suffers a heart attack, newly qualified
doctor Jamie agrees to act as a locum at his general practice.
Jon's partner, Dr Sam Paige, is not convinced she's up to the
job. Her first priority is to prove herself and then make him
realise she's a woman too! But is she too late…

FALLING FOR A STRANGER by Janet Ferguson

For ward sister Anna Chancellor, returning to work after
what should have been her honeymoon was very hard.
Being jilted made her feel she couldn't trust love again.
Orthopaedic Registrar Daniel Mackay's disastrous marriage
made him feel the same way. Can they dispense with
caution and accept the love they've found?

Available from 2nd June 2000

FREE!

4 Books
and a surprise gift!

We would like to take this opportunity to thank you for reading this Mills & Boon® book by offering you the chance to take FOUR more specially selected titles from the Medical Romance™ series absolutely FREE! We're also making this offer to introduce you to the benefits of the Reader Service™—

- ★ FREE home delivery
- ★ FREE gifts and competitions
- ★ FREE monthly Newsletter
- ★ Books available before they're in the shops
- ★ Exclusive Reader Service discounts

Accepting these FREE books and gift places you under no obligation to buy; you may cancel at any time, even after receiving your free shipment. Simply complete your details below and return the entire page to the address below. *You don't even need a stamp!*

YES! Please send me 4 free Medical Romance books and a surprise gift. I understand that unless you hear from me, I will receive 6 superb new titles every month for just £2.40 each, postage and packing free. I am under no obligation to purchase any books and may cancel my subscription at any time. The free books and gift will be mine to keep in any case.

M0EB

Ms/Mrs/Miss/Mr ....Initials..............................
BLOCK CAPITALS PLEASE

Surname...

Address..

....

....Postcode ....

Send this whole page to:
UK: The Reader Service, FREEPOST CN81, Croydon, CR9 3WZ
EIRE: The Reader Service, PO Box 4546, Kilcock, County Kildare (stamp required)

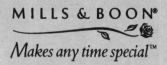

MILLS & BOON®

Makes any time special™

COMING SOON

St. Elizabeth's
Children's Hospital

A limited collection of 12 books. Where affairs of
the heart are entwined with the everyday dealings
of this warm and friendly children's hospital.

Book 1
A Winter Bride by Meredith Webber
Published 5th May